W9-DAS-301

"Our marriage of convenience ended at six o'clock this morning."

Gabe continued. "A limo will be by for you in two hours. You've got your tickets? Everything?"

Stefanie smiled. "You don't have to worry about me anymore. I took care of myself before we met, and can do so again."

Gabe sobered. "I realize that. But after a year of being your husband, I find I'm still in the habit." He paused. "Then I guess this is goodbye. Thank you for everything, Stefanie. I'll never forget you."

After giving her a kiss on her petal-smooth cheek, Gabe left the study, aware of a haunting sense of loss. That was something he hadn't expected....

To have and to hold...

Their marriage was meant to last—
and they have the gold rings to prove it!

To love and to cherish...

But what happens when their promise
to love, honor and cherish is put to the test?

From this day forward...

Emotions run high as husbands and wives discover
how precious—and fragile—their wedding vows are....
Will true love keep them together—forever?

Marriages meant to last!

Look out in September for
The Marriage Test (#3669)
by Barbara McMahon

HUSBAND FOR A YEAR

Rebecca Winters

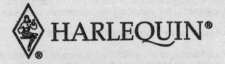

TORONTO • NEW YORK • LONDON
AMSTERDAM • PARIS • SYDNEY • HAMBURG
STOCKHOLM • ATHENS • TOKYO • MILAN • MADRID
PRAGUE • WARSAW • BUDAPEST • AUCKLAND

ISBN 0-373-03665-5

HUSBAND FOR A YEAR

First North American Publication 2001.

Copyright © 2001 by Rebecca Winters.

Visit us at www.eHarlequin.com

Printed in U.S.A.

CHAPTER ONE

GABE stared at the serenely beautiful woman seated across the desk from him. For as long as he'd known her, people had commented that she was a new version of the legendary blond princess, Grace Kelly. He agreed there was a superficial likeness in looks and style.

Women envied her and always would.

Men envied him for having exclusive rights to her company. One day the whole world would admire her.

"Stefanie? As you're well aware, our marriage of convenience ended at six o'clock this morning. There must have been times when you thought March 28 would never come around."

She crossed one long, elegant leg over the other in a totally feminine gesture. "Let's agree that both of us have been anxious for this day to arrive."

He nodded. "Our annulment means you can go back to being Stefanie Dawson, this state's most attractive and sought-after young socialite. Now that you're free to get on with the rest of your life, men, young and old, will line up to win your heart. Some very lucky man is going to succeed."

Her china-blue eyes smiled. "You think?"

His lips twitched. "I *know*. You'll probably meet him before the year is out. Maybe even on your trip around the world. Are you packed and ready to go?"

"Yes."

"A limo will be by for you in two hours. You've got your tickets? Everything?"

She smiled. "You don't have to worry about me anymore. I took care of myself before we met, and shall do so again."

He sobered. "I realize that. But after a year of being your husband, I find I'm still in the habit."

"Once out of sight, out of mind." Her glib response was oddly disturbing.

Shifting his weight he said, "For the record, you've fulfilled your end of the bargain far beyond my expectations. Your reward is in this envelope, but no financial compensation could ever be enough to express the depth of my gratitude for your sacrifice. I'll always be indebted to you. If you want, we can go over the settlement now."

"I don't. When you give your word, I've learned you keep it."

There was fire in her remark. Fire he hadn't expected.

"Then I guess this is goodbye." Pushing the leather chair away from the desk, he got to his feet and walked around to her. The enticing floral fragrance he associated with her filled his nostrils.

"Thank you for everything, Stefanie. You're a remarkable woman who deserves all that life has to offer. There's no one like you. I'll never forget."

After giving her a kiss on her petal-smooth cheek, he left the study, aware of a haunting sense of loss. That, too, was something he hadn't expected...

Stefanie waited until she heard the front door close before running over to the window. The driver put Gabe's suitcase in the trunk, but she kept her eyes on the tall, dark-haired male who was taking her heart with him. Exquisite pain smote her when he levered himself in the back seat without once turning his head for a final look of farewell.

A year ago today Gabe's father, the powerful Senator Hershal Wainwright of Rhode Island, had gotten what he wanted—a new daughter-in-law—the one he'd handpicked to be Gabe's wife. Two months after their marriage, the senator had gotten something else he wanted—reelection to a fifth term in the U.S. Senate.

Today, Gabriel Wainwright, the senator's fourth and youngest son, the handsome, hands-down public favorite of all the Wainwright sons, the one with the most promise, brilliance, charisma and charm, the one whom people, including the senator, insisted would end up in the White House one day, got what he wanted—freedom from a temporary marriage which had served its purpose—freedom to leave the past behind and live according to the dictates of his own conscience.

Both men had gotten exactly what they wanted. Now it was Stefanie's turn...

Her first order of business was to cancel the limo Gabe had requested for her. With that accomplished, she spent the rest of the day finalizing certain secret plans of her own.

At seven that evening, dressed in a champagne silk suit designed by her favorite French couturier Fabrice, she entered the Newport Yacht Club where her father was commodore.

Turning heads with every graceful step, she found the headwaiter. After asking him to hold dinner until she gave the signal, she breezed through to the private dining room where she'd invited her parents and Gabe's to help celebrate their first wedding anniversary. As usual, the four of them were deep in conversation over political matters.

Since Senator Wainwright's reelection, he'd been pushing for Stefanie's father, who sat on the Federal Reserve Board, to consider accepting the appointment as Secretary of the Treasury, if it was offered. The former secretary had recently died, leaving a vacancy in the cabinet.

"Good evening, everyone." She made her round of the table, accepting and giving compliments and kisses. Gabe's father proffered an extra hug. He'd never made a secret of his feelings where she was concerned. Unfortunately, when he heard what she had to say, it would probably be his last demonstration of affection toward her.

After Stefanie reached her place, she remained standing.

"Before dinner is served, I have an important announcement to make."

"Oh, darling!" her mother cried for happiness. By now both sets of parents were beaming. "Don't you want to wait for your husband to finish parking the car before you give us your exciting news?"

If it weren't so vital, Stefanie would never purposely hurt either family like this. They were so certain she was going to tell them a new little Wainwright was on the way.

"He's not coming, Mother."

Something in her tone sounded serious enough to erase their smiles. The festive air in the room evaporated.

She'd had all day to practice this speech, but

there'd been no audience to listen to it. Now she was the focus of four pairs of eyes all regarding her with varying degrees of anxiety.

Forgive me, Gabe. What I'm about to do wasn't part of your plan, but I love you too much to let you walk out of my life without a fight.

"As all of you know, seventeen months ago Gabe asked me out to dinner. When I came home, I was wearing his engagement ring. Five months later we were married. But I've never told any of you the details of that evening. Now it's time to reveal them."

"You sound so serious," her mother wailed.

Stefanie swallowed hard, trying to tamp down the pain. "Please—just hear me out. All of you."

Her father nodded. "We're listening, sweetheart."

"Thank you. After dinner was served, Gabe asked me a question. He said, 'Is it true what Father says, that you hope to end up in the White House as First Lady one day?'"

She stared at Gabe's father. "Your son's question caught me off guard because I knew I'd never said such a thing to you or anyone else."

The senator cleared his throat. "That was wishful thinking on the part of an old man who happens to love you very much, Stefanie," he muttered.

His confession would have pleased her if it hadn't done so much damage. "I had no idea. The thing is, I was so in love with Gabe, so overjoyed to be out with him, I teasingly blurted back, 'Isn't it *every* woman's dream?'"

"Look, my dear—" the senator started to say, but she preempted him.

"Please allow me to continue. Gabe studied me

thoughtfully, then said, 'In that case I have a proposition for you.' At that point I was confused because I thought he'd been leading up to a marriage proposal. But I couldn't have been further from the truth.

"In a businesslike tone he confessed that he'd reached the place in his life where it was necessary to marry the right woman for a temporary period. His use of the word 'temporary' dashed my dreams."

Their collective gasps resounded in the private dining room.

"While I sat there reeling in pain, he explained that this woman would have to be a high-profile person who, as his wife, could legitimately fill in for him in public from time to time while he was away undertaking certain activities he didn't want anyone to know about."

"What activities?" The senator had gotten his wild-eyed look.

"Let me finish." She paused to catch her breath. "G-Gabe said that, at a time when his father was making another bid for the senate and deserved to run a worry-free campaign, he knew marriage to me would fulfill his parents' dream."

"Surely they were *his* dreams, too!" his mother cried.

Stefanie loved her mother-in-law for that outburst, but she shook her head. "No. Then he spelled out the terms. He said that if I agreed to marry him, our marriage would last for one year, a-and be in name only. On March 28, it would be legally annulled."

"That son of mine must have had some kind of breakdown!"

"Not Gabe," she whispered sadly. "For my cooperation, I would receive a generous financial settlement that would make me independently wealthy in my own right, and I would walk away as pure as the day I had entered the marriage. Furthermore I would be free to marry a man whose whole desire was to take me to the White House with him.''

While they sat there in frozen shock, she decided she'd better go on while she still could.

"As you know, today is March 28. Gabe's been living for it." Her voice shook. "Early this morning he left the house to embark on his new life, whatever that is. He won't be coming back."

The senator glowered at her. "If this is his idea of a joke, we're not amused."

"Neither am I," she whispered in agony.

Gabe's father's eyes showed confusion, a rare sight. "What do you mean, not coming back? He has a law firm to run! Among other things, I'm throwing some new projects his way that will be vital to his future political career!"

She shook her head. "You haven't been listening to me. For the past few months he's been turning over his cases to other colleagues in the firm so he could leave without problem. When the time is right, he'll contact you, but I presume that won't be for a while."

"Nonsense!"

Stefanie ignored the senator's angry exclamation.

"In order not to embarrass either family, he prepared his office and house staff by telling them that because we've been in the spotlight so much since our marriage, he and I are going on a trip around the world which could last six months."

Again the four people in the room stared at her in stunned disbelief.

"He explained about the trip in letters he sent to you," she continued. "You'll receive them in the mail tomorrow." She cleared her throat. "If I had carried out his plans to the letter, I would be in Paris right now enjoying the first stop of my long holiday. But as you can see, I chose not to go because—"

"Enough!" Now it was her father who shoved himself away from the table and jumped to his feet. As he threw down his napkin, it caused his wineglass to topple. "A marriage in name only—I've never heard such rubbish in all my life! How dare Gabe do this to you! How *dare* he!"

She'd never seen him so angry. "Dad—please sit down. I'm not through."

"What's wrong with our son?" Gabe's mother sounded on the verge of hysteria as she cried to her husband, pulling on his arm.

Stefanie's mother shook her head in despair. "I can't believe this has happened. I simply can't believe it! Stefanie—aside from his despicable actions, whatever possessed *you* to say yes to such a cold-blooded proposition? Heavens, darling, you could have married *any* man you wanted!"

A tight band constricted Stefanie's breathing. "I didn't want any man, Mom. I wanted Gabe. When I was an adolescent, I developed a painful crush that never went away. After ten years of loving him, I would have married him for any reason," her voice throbbed.

"Fool that I am, I'd convinced myself that once we lived together, he would tear up that wretched contract and make our marriage real. But I learned that you can't force someone to fall in love with you. Since we'd made a contract, I didn't dare try to dissuade him from his plans."

"*What* plans?" The senator's rage was starting to escalate out of control.

"I have no idea," she answered honestly. "He'll have to be the one to reveal them—when he's ready."

A ruddy color stained his cheeks. "Where *is* my son?"

"I don't know yet, but I'm working on it."

"You mean he's really gone?" Gabe's father still couldn't comprehend it. For that matter, neither could Stefanie.

"Yes. But I—I hired a P.I. to follow him."

"Thank God you had that much sense!" came the senator's furious outburst.

Her father shook his head. "The idea of his marrying you to provide a smokescreen for secret activities is preposterous! What kind of a man would use a woman like that? Especially when she's my precious daughter!"

Before everything exploded in her face, Stefanie needed to get this over with. "Don't blame Gabe. I'm the one who said yes to his proposition. *Think for a minute*—

"He could have been selfish and disappeared right in the middle of the reelection campaign. It would have caused you untold grief and pain. But he didn't do that. Instead he planned everything to ensure his actions would prevent any scandal.

"Don't you see? No matter how hurt all of you are, no matter how this may look to you, Gabe's the most honorable man I've ever known in my life."

"Honorable?" her father blurted. "He took advantage of your vulnerability and broke your heart!"

"But *he* doesn't know that, Dad."

"What do you mean?"

"I—I never told him how I felt, not when I realized he wasn't in love with me. Behind closed doors we lived totally separate lives. He believed I was happy with our arrangement."

Her mother shook her head. "How could he be so blind?"

"Because I never disabused him of the assumption he made about my wanting a husband who would end up in the Oval Office! Mom—he has no idea he's the only man I'll ever love. That's why I'm not taking the world tour he planned for me.

"As soon as I find out his destination, then I'll act on that knowledge and go after him with a proposition of my own!"

The senator shot out of his chair. He stopped pacing the floor long enough to blurt, "This is *your* fault, Stefanie. You should have told me the truth about your marriage months ago so I could have prevented this tragedy from happening. Whatever you have to do, I want him home by the end of the week where he belongs!"

"You don't want him back as much as I do," she said, standing her ground. "But it's not going to be easy. Gabe's no longer my husband. When he said goodbye this morning, he meant it to be forever. He trusted me...

"What I'm about to do could backfire in ways I don't even want to contemplate. In fact the thought of facing him terrifies me. But it's a risk I *have* to take—'' She struggled for breath. ''B-because life isn't worth living without him.''

The senator stood there with his jaw clenched. For the first time since she'd known him, he was powerless to do anything.

But he wouldn't stay helpless for long. As she knew only too well, his tentacles reached many places. When he wanted something, he was virtually unstoppable. More than ever she understood why Gabe would have reached a total impasse with his father a long time ago. A shiver ran down her spine.

''I'm going to need everyone's help,'' she continued. ''For the time being you'll have to pretend to go along with Gabe's and my story about our trip. Will you do that for us?''

Her father's eyes had grown bleak. ''If you're determined about this, it doesn't look like we have any other choice.''

''Thank you, Dad. I promise to stay in touch with all of you. Now if you'll excuse me—''

''No, Stefanie!'' Her mother knocked over her chair getting up from the table. ''You can't leave yet, darling!''

''I have to go, Mom. The limo is waiting. I told the P.I. to phone me at nine. I want to be home when the call comes through. It may take several days, even longer, before I know exactly where Gabe went. Then I can make my plans. In the meantime, I'm counting on you to pretend everything's fine. That's what Gabe wanted.''

The senator pinned her with a withering gaze, the kind he used for intimidating people he didn't like. He didn't like her anymore. In placing her loyalty to Gabe above his father, she'd dropped from favor.

It was very sad because there were qualities about him she'd grown to love by virtue of his being her father-in-law. He'd also done a great deal of humanitarian good in the world.

"I'm expecting you to bring my son to his senses, Stefanie." Though he didn't add the words "or else," his warning was unmistakable.

Gabe's father was afraid. So was she...

Blowing everyone a kiss, she hurried through the club and out the front doors to the limo which was waiting for her.

"Drive me to the Oyster Inn, please. I'm meeting friends there. They'll take me home later."

"Very good, Mrs. Wainwright."

As soon as they reached the popular restaurant in downtown Newport, the chauffeur helped her out, then drove off. Left to her own devices, Stefanie walked to the end of the street and rounded the corner.

Earlier in the day she'd paid cash for a used car, which sat parked at the curb. Her new cell phone was packed in one of the suitcases she'd stashed in the trunk. After retrieving it, plus a wig with short black curls styled like a Gypsy's, she climbed in behind the wheel of the small blue compact.

With her shoulder-length hair worn up, she could easily slip on the wig. Once it was in place she started the engine, anxious to put as many miles between her and Newport as possible.

The senator might still be at the club with his wife and her parents, but she had no doubts he'd already excused himself long enough to order a surveillance team to set up a watch outside the fabulous

Nantucket shingle house Gabe had given her for a wedding present.

Before long there would be a tap on her home phone. Gabe's father would have her every move scrutinized until she led him to his son.

While she'd been married to Gabe, she'd learned a lot about the senator that hadn't been apparent when she'd first gone to work for his reelection campaign two years earlier.

Senator Wainwright was a dynasty builder. His sons were his possessions. His word, law. Though he adored his children, he would consider it unconscionable for one of them to defect from the family. Especially Gabe, whom he privately favored.

What his youngest son had done today was tantamount to high treason. Unthinkable. Unforgivable. She'd seen it in his father's eyes. He would stop at nothing to bring Gabe back to the fold, even if it meant spying on Stefanie in her own home.

But she had the element of surprise on her side. By the time he realized she'd outsmarted him, she would be over state lines and impossible to trace.

The call she'd been waiting for came at 9:00 p.m. exactly. Her heart hammered as she clicked on and said hello.

"Ms. Dawson?"

"Yes, Wes! What news do you have for me?"

"Your ex-husband flew to Providence by shuttle, then left the airport in a half-ton pickup truck with Montana license plates."

Montana?

She'd thought he might have been planning to fly overseas in a private jet. "W-was there someone with him?" *Please don't tell me it was a woman.*

"Not at first."

Oh, no.

"But before he left the city, he stopped off at a very fancy military academy to pick up a boy and a woman."

She let out a gasp of surprise. "Did you get a good look at them?"

"Yes. I'd say the boy is fourteen or fifteen years old, fairly tall for his age. On the lean side, dark-haired. The brunette woman looked anywhere from her mid-thirties to mid-forties. Attractive."

Dear God— Could the boy be Gabe's son? Was that the great secret he'd been keeping from everyone? If so, was the woman his mother? Was Gabe taking them away? Did he love her?

Stefanie was in so much pain, she could hardly breathe.

"Ms. Dawson?"

"Y-yes?"

"Okay. I was just checking to make sure you were still on the line. Stan and I have tailed them to Erie, Pennsylvania, where they've pulled into a motel parking lot. I'm assuming they'll stay here for the night."

Gabe was in Erie? That meant he'd been driving nonstop since he'd picked up his passengers. It was one thing to fear that he might have been seeing another women throughout their marriage. But the knowledge that he was actually with her at a motel right now almost destroyed Stefanie.

"Stan is going to relieve me so I can get some sleep in the back of the van. You've got his cell phone number. Call him whenever you want an update."

"Thank you. I—I will," she murmured, her voice

shaking with fear that Gabe had been in love with the woman all these years. Someone his family wouldn't have liked?

If that was the case, then it was no wonder he'd never broken the terms of that wretched contract he'd made with Stefanie. He'd had no desire to make love to her when the mother of his son was out there waiting for him to be free.

Stefanie stifled her moan, not knowing what to think. "Please—don't lose sight of him," she begged. "Right now I'm in my car following you."

"We've never lost a target yet."

"Whatever you do, don't let him see you! You have to understand he doesn't want to be found."

"I'm aware of that. At this point you're going to have to trust us to get the job done. We always do."

She bit her lip. "I pray you're right. I'll make it worth your while."

"You already have. I promise he won't get away from us."

"Then I guess I can't ask for more than that." Stefanie clicked off, terrified something could still go wrong and she'd never see Gabe again.

Another hour and her eyelids started to droop. At the next sign for lodgings she pulled off the freeway and drove to a Cozy Inn for the night. Once settled, she climbed into bed and made another phone call. Gabe was still at the same motel. With her…

After thanking Stan for the information, she buried her face in the pillow. It was wet by the time she fell into oblivion.

"This is going to be so cool, Gabe."

"You think?"

Gabe smiled as he eyed the fifteen-year-old seated in the cab of his truck. Every time he'd visited with Clay Talbot in the past, the troubled boy Gabe had influenced the court to send to the tightly enforced military academy rather than a state correctional facility, he had grown on him a little more.

"Yeah. I can't believe we're almost there."

"You realize this is only an experiment."

"I know."

"You've been released to my custody. If you don't obey the rules, my hands will be tied and the court will send you back to the academy."

"I hated that place. It might as well have been a prison."

"Take my word for it, the academy doesn't come close to the real thing."

After a long silence, "I swear I'm not going to get into trouble again."

"I hope not, Clay. It would disappoint me and break your mom's heart. But more importantly, you would be letting yourself down."

The boy nodded his dark head.

At least there'd been some side benefits to this trip. For one thing, Clay and his mom had been able to share some precious time together before he'd dropped her off at the airport in Chicago for the flight back to Providence.

Being an alcoholic, it was as far as she could travel without wanting a drink. Gabe had made it clear there would be no alcohol during the trip. He'd challenged her to handle it long enough to connect with the son she hadn't seen in months. Though she'd been unable to make it all the way to Montana, Clay seemed okay with it.

As for Gabe, he'd had an opportunity to get inside Clay's head. Enough time to establish a tentative rapport with the teen who'd been born of affluent parents who didn't know the first thing about child rearing.

Unfortunately the death of Clay's father to cancer two years earlier had turned his world upside down. Unable to deal with his own pain, let alone that of his grieving alcoholic mother, he'd gotten into trouble with other kids from wealthy Providence homes who could afford drugs and were indiscriminately vandalizing their exclusive neighborhoods for the fun of it.

In desperation, Clay's mother had finally retained Gabe to defend her son in court. But sending the boy to military school had only been a stopgap. Now that Gabe was free to live his destiny, hopefully Clay would receive the emotional and psychological help he desperately needed.

As they continued driving through old snow, a familiar road sign showed up on the right.

Welcome To Marion, Montana. You're In God's Country Now.

Gabe had passed it dozens of times over the last year. It meant their long drive across the U.S. was about to come to an end.

Before this trip he'd always flown to Glacier Park International Airport where his foreman, Mack Whittaker, waited to take him back to the ranch in the station wagon.

Not this time.

It didn't take a prophet to know that all hell had broken loose now that both families had received the

letters Gabe had posted. Even though he'd told his
parents he had gone abroad, there was still a chance
his father would try and find him. Gabe had chosen
to come by truck in order not to leave a trail.

In a couple of months he would write another set
of letters explaining that he and Stefanie had gone
their separate ways.

Thankfully she'd flown to Paris a few hours after
he'd left the house and was enjoying herself with
good friends as planned.

Now that she'd been given her freedom, she was
entitled to be with any man she chose. To Gabe's
chagrin, he found he loathed the idea. Her image, her
husky voice, had refused to leave his mind or senses.

He supposed she would haunt him for a long time
to come. You didn't live for a year in the same house
with a wife like Stefanie and hope to walk away from
her totally unaffected.

On the other hand, he hadn't realized how deeply
she'd gotten beneath his skin. The drive through a
lot of rain and some snow flurries would have been
torture if he'd had to be alone with his thoughts.

He figured it would probably take hearing that
Stefanie was going to marry someone else's favorite
son headed for the White House to douse the sparks
Gabe had determined not to acknowledge, let alone
allow to catch fire.

His face formed a grimace before he gunned the
accelerator. Twenty minutes later he glimpsed something in the twilight that broke his torturous train of
thought.

Larch Tree Boys' Ranch.

When Gabe saw the newly erected sign at the gate,

he let out a satisfied sigh and slowed down. Mack must have pulled some strings to make sure it had been put up in time to coincide with Gabe's arrival.

A special welcome home present.

The best one he could have received to chase away feelings that were better left to die.

When he and the Realtor from Kalispell had flown over this property eighteen months ago, everything about the ranch had felt right to him. Seventy-five thousand acres of lush green meadows dotted with cattle and statuesque pines.

In the early-morning sunlight he'd glimpsed a ribbon of blue teeming with trout as it danced against a dense green forest backdrop. A couple of rustic log cabins nestled here and there in a fertile valley surrounded by snow-capped mountains completed a picture that spoke straight to Gabe's restless soul.

Always before, his needs, aspirations and desires had been fragmented, eluding him like some flirtatious breeze he couldn't follow. Then he'd seen the ranch and suddenly everything had crystallized for him.

It was here he would put down roots.

The ranch was the one special spot on earth that called to him, and heaven knew he and his family had seen and traveled more of mother earth than most people.

"This is it?" Clay cried out excitedly.

"Yes. We're home."

But with Stefanie no longer in the picture, the word had a hollow ring. That was a reality Gabe was going to have to live with.

Shifting gears, he drove the truck onto his private

property. Though it was early spring, the place looked like winter had still gotten in a few final licks.

"How come you didn't name the ranch after you?"

"The larch trees were here first, not the Wainwrights. Now I hope you're hungry because I can promise that Marva will have her famous home-made chili waiting for us."

"Is she your wife?"

Gabe took a deep breath before he said, "No. She's the cook for the main ranch house."

"Mom showed me a picture of Mrs. Wainwright from the newspaper. She's *really* good looking!"

"I agree." Gabe's voice grated. If the truth be known, Stefanie was probably the most beautiful woman he'd ever seen in his life.

"Is she already at the ranch?"

His hands tightened on the steering wheel. "No."

"When's she going to come?"

"She's *not,* Clay. Right now she's on a trip around the world."

The boy frowned. "Why?"

He rubbed the side of his unshaven jaw. "She needed time away on her own."

Clay looked at him with a solemn expression. "Are you two getting a divorce?"

He'd been asked an honest question. To hedge it would only provoke more curiosity.

"We *are* divorced."

"Didn't she want to live on a ranch?"

"It was more a case of her wanting to live the life she loves on the East Coast."

"Did she ever see your ranch?"

Perspiration formed on Gabe's brow. "No."

"But that's crazy! She'd only have to get one look at this place, and she'd never want to go back!"

Gabe shook his head. *To be young again. To see life in such a simplistic way.* "It's never going to happen."

"That's too bad." The boy was still mourning his father's death. Saying goodbye to Stefanie didn't seem to be that much different for Gabe...

"As you've already been made painfully aware, life doesn't always go the way we want. What do you say we both put the past behind us and move forward from here?"

The boy's head was bowed. "That's kind of hard to do, but I'll try if you will."

Once more Gabe's heart went out to Clay. He patted his shoulder. "It's a deal."

CHAPTER TWO

STEFANIE spent a restless night in Kalispell, Montana. Though the woman riding with Gabe had been dropped off at O'Hare airport in Chicago, Stefanie's dreams were still haunted by the reality of her existence and the possibility that Gabe was in love with her.

Heartsick, Stefanie drove on to the tiny hamlet of Marion where she'd been told to meet the P.I.s at the coffee shop of the Branding Iron motel.

The rustic little café bar appeared deserted, no doubt because a weather report forecasting a storm before evening had prompted tourists to run for cover while they could.

By now it was ten after three. After two hours of watching for Stan and Wes out of antler-trimmed windows, she was convinced something had gone wrong. To come this far only to lose Gabe's trail was anathema to her.

When she finally spotted their rental van, she left the booth and ran to the entrance to meet them.

"You can relax," Wes assured her as they walked back to her table. "The boys' ranch where your ex-husband spent last night is his final destination."

The waitress took orders for hot coffee.

Bewildered by the information, Stefanie asked, "How do you know that for certain?"

"I made a phone call, pretending to be a parent wanting information," Stan explained. "According to the woman who answered, the combination ranch and accredited school for teenaged boys in trouble with the law is the brain child of a Mr. Wainwright, the owner and manager.''

What?

''To quote her words, 'The structured environment of his working cattle ranch offers a viable alternative to the usual punitive reform school. The boys live, study and work on the ranch in family groups with trained counselors, teachers and surrogate parents. The result is a much higher rate of rehabilitated young men who will make positive contributions to society in the future.'''

Stefanie shook her head trying to assimilate everything Stan had just told her, but she couldn't fathom it.

Gabe had turned his back on a political career, which could have taken him to the highest office in the land in order to live in this remote, savage wilderness surrounded by young criminals?

Throughout the endless drive across the country, she'd become convinced that Gabe's passenger was his son, that he and the boy's mother were going to end up here together.

Maybe that still held true. It was possible the woman he loved would be joining him later.

Stefanie felt her heart splinter.

Having learned this much, would it be unforgivable of her to show up at the ranch? While they'd been married, Gabe had had many months to tell her the truth, but she'd waited in vain for him to confide in her.

While she struggled with these questions, Wes placed a Montana map in front of her. ''This is the way to the Larch Tree Boys' Ranch, Ms. Dawson. I've highlighted the route in blue. Weather permitting, it's a twenty-minute drive from here."

"I'll never be able to thank you enough for what you've done." Stefanie handed them both a bonus check.

"We were glad to be of help." Stan smiled. "Good luck to you."

"To you, too."

"Thanks. Let us know if we can ever be of help again."

"You know I will."

The P.I.s had done their part to perfection. She'd been given the proof that Gabe wasn't going anywhere. He wasn't lost to her. But she'd been so focused on catching up to him, she hadn't thought beyond this moment.

After the two men left the café for Kalispell, Stefanie searched her conscience. No matter how she analyzed it, there was no right way to approach Gabe. In his eyes she would be an unwelcome intruder, a tangible reminder of the life he'd repudiated.

Worse, there was the reality of the woman who'd driven partway across the country with Gabe and the boy who could be his son, thus complicating an already precarious situation.

What caused Stefanie to agonize was not knowing if Gabe was in love—whether it be with the boy's mother, or whether he was involved with another woman altogether.

There was no one who could help her get those answers.

Unless she abandoned her hope of ever seeing

Gabe again, the only thing left to do was carry out her original plan. At this point she had nothing else to lose.

If her worst nightmare came true and Gabe ended up despising her, at least she wouldn't spend the rest of her life torturing herself with *what ifs*.

Determined as she'd never been in her life, she went into the rest room to make certain no blond strands had escaped her wig. Then she refreshed her makeup. It had been carefully chosen to camouflage her fair coloring and play up her black hair. With brown contact lenses, gold hoop earrings, a black turtleneck sweater and designer jeans, her own mother wouldn't recognize her.

That was the whole point.

Gabe had led a double life for months. Except for the P.I.s who'd been paid well for their silence, not to mention their help, only the people involved with his ranch knew where he was. Stefanie had no intention of giving his secret away. In fact she'd done everything in her power to make sure no one would suspect she was the former Mrs. Gabriel Wainwright.

After taking a deep breath, she went out front to pay for her lunch. It wasn't until she started for her car that she realized a wind had sprung up. Snow had been forecast.

With the ranch only twenty minutes away, she estimated that if she drove there immediately, she could make it without problem. Otherwise she might have to wait another day to see Gabe, depending on the severity of the storm.

When she'd come this far, it didn't bear thinking about to be so close and still have to put off a reunion with him. She'd lived through five days and nights with the fear that something would go wrong and she'd never be able to find him. Now that she was within a few miles of his ranch, she couldn't get there fast enough.

By the time the image of the motel had disappeared from her rearview mirror, the rain had turned to snow which was pelting the windshield. She turned on the wipers. Over the past few hours there'd been a noticeable drop in temperature. Twice she'd had to slow down because of black ice.

In this lonely wilderness, she found it hard to believe it was early April. Even more difficult to understand was Gabe's decision to lose himself out here.

Anyone acquainted with the Wainwright sons knew they were expert swimmers and sailors. Certainly Gabe was one with the sea. Besides water sports, he loved offshore fishing. The rougher the swells and battering of salt spray, the better.

Stefanie was a water baby herself. Throughout their brief marriage she'd shared many of those activities with him, but always in the company of others.

For those reasons, she couldn't imagine what had drawn him to this landlocked backcountry with no ocean in sight. No yachts or sailboats. No people.

The more she surveyed these hostile surroundings, the more incredulous she grew that this was a permanent move on his part.

"Oh, Gabe—what are you really doing out here?" she cried in anguish. *"Why?"*

At first she thought it was only the tears blurring her eyes that hampered her vision. But after she'd traveled the required distance and still couldn't find the gate to the ranch, she realized she'd been over-taken by the blizzard.

Without being able to see one inch in front of her, there was no other choice but to pull to the side of the road and wait until the worst of the storm had passed over.

The next thing she knew, the car tipped forward and came to a standstill in a ditch. Though it wasn't terribly deep, she would have been thrown against the windshield if she hadn't been wearing a seat belt.

Everything went quiet. No sound of the engine, no heater. In this whiteout she'd completely lost her bearings.

Once her nerves calmed down and she got herself under some semblance of control, she forced herself to think rationally. If the storm kept up, and it probably would for some time to come, she might be stranded here for hours. Maybe all night. No one would know she'd gone off the road.

On the other hand, if she got out of the car and tried to find Gabe on foot, she could be hit by another car, or come down with hypothermia. The only thing that made sense was to call 911 and hope she was in range for someone to answer. Unfortunately her purse had been thrown to the floor.

Due to the odd angle of the car, she had a struggle undoing the seat belt. Eventually she worked it free, then clung to the steering wheel with one hand while she reached for her handbag with the other. After some difficulty she fished out her cell phone and punched the digits.

"Sheriff's office," a robust male voice answered. *Thank heaven.*

"H-hello? I'm—" She hesitated, realizing she'd

almost said Stefanie Wainwright. "T-this is Teri Jones. I've run off the road into a ditch near the gate to the Larch Tree Boys' Ranch. At least that's where I was headed after I left Marion."

"Are you injured, ma'am?"

"No. Just anxious."

"What kind of a car are you driving?"

"It's a dark blue 1989 Honda Civic."

"Stay put. In this kind of weather you never know what's moving out there." Stefanie shivered, wondering if the man was talking about wild animals, like a bear or something. "We'll get help to you as fast as we can."

She swallowed her fear. "Thank you so much."

When Gabe's cell phone rang, he'd been riding through fresh snow in the lower pasture, checking to make sure there was enough feed for the herd. No one from the ranch house would be bothering him during this blizzard unless it was important.

He reined in his horse, then pulled the phone from his jacket. Another gust of snow forced him to lower the tip of his Stetson as a shield so he could be heard.

"Gabe here."

"Gabe? It's Marva. A minute ago the sheriff's office phoned the main house. Apparently a woman named Teri Jones, driving a blue Honda, is stranded on the road near the gate to the ranch, but it seems all police rescue vehicles are out on emergencies right now. Since they're shorthanded, the dispatcher wondered if somebody around here could investigate. Whom shall I send?"

His horse pranced in place. Every available stockman and ranch hand, including Mack, were checking for strays in the other pastures, making sure there was plenty of feed. Gabe realized he was probably closest to the main road.

"I'll see about it. Keep the coffee hot."

"You bet."

"Thanks, Marva." He slipped the phone back in place. "Let's go home."

He hurried back to the barn where he asked one of the hands to take care of Caesar. Within minutes he'd climbed in the Explorer. Fortunately in that short amount of time the wind had died down and the worst of the blizzard seemed to have passed over.

One thing about the early spring storms. They didn't last long. A strong sun had been making inroads on the snowdrifts built up over the winter. Large patches of green meadow were springing up everywhere. He'd even seen some yellow primroses at the higher elevations, pushing through the ice. The sight had been glorious.

Still, the sun was nowhere to be found right now. He imagined the stranded woman was wondering if help would ever arrive. It was past dinnertime. If she hadn't planned for an emergency, she was probably hungry and frightened.

The seven-mile drive to the gate through the wet virgin snow presented little problem. But after reaching the main road, he didn't see a sign of a car or any tire tracks. Deciding to take a right, he proceeded in that direction for a couple of miles. When nothing showed up, he turned around and headed back the other way.

A mile past the gate he spotted a snow-covered vehicle, which had gone into the ditch headfirst. He pulled up alongside and turned on his hazard light.

Still keeping the engine running, he levered himself from the seat and walked over to the car.

"Ms. Jones?" After knocking on the left rear window to announce his arrival, he climbed into the shallow culvert. With a gloved hand, he started removing snow from the driver's window so he could see inside. Before he'd finished the job, the glass slid down.

"Thank you for coming!" she cried with undisguised relief.

For a brief moment his eyes glimpsed the profile of a stunning woman with short, glossy black curls. Combined with her husky voice, he was strongly reminded of someone else whose beauty had taken his breath the first time he'd ever laid eyes on her.

He thought he must be hallucinating until she turned to face him. The seductive floral scent that had enticed him on too many other occasions drifted past him.

Her makeup and earrings might be different, the brown lenses fake, but he'd know the bewitching lines of that exquisite face and mouth anywhere.

The blood pounded in his ears.

"Stefanie?"

"Yes," came her terrified whisper. Beneath the makeup, her complexion had paled. "Please don't be angry with me, Gabe. *Please.*" Her gently rounded chin quivered. "You have to hear me out! No one knows I'm here. Your secret is safe. I swear it!"

He was so shocked to see her, the meaning of her words didn't register right away. All this time he'd imagined her in Paris, charming every damn male in sight.

His gaze followed the involuntary movement of

her hand to her heart, drawing his attention to the gorgeous mold of her body. The black sweater proved faithful to her rounded curves.

"How in the hell did you find me?"

Even to his own ears he knew he sounded furious, but he felt out of control, unable to quell the myriad of conflicting emotions that were exploding inside him.

She moistened her luscious red mouth nervously. The color was one she'd never worn before. The sight of it on her lips was incredibly erotic. "I—I had you followed. But don't worry!" she blurted. "They'll never tell anyone."

He fought not to erupt again, but it was almost impossible. "Who are *they?*" he demanded in a deceptively silky tone.

She swallowed hard, once again distracting him as his gaze studied the creamy column of her throat rising out of the material. No woman in the world had such flawless skin.

"A team of p-private detectives. I paid them well."

"What's this all about, Stefanie?" He fired the question before he noticed she'd been gripping the steering wheel to keep from falling sideways. When he realized how she was straining, he yanked the door open and pulled her out.

Obviously unprepared, she fell against him like a rag doll, leaving the imprint of her beautiful body against his, turning his legs leaden until his breathing constricted.

Though he knew it was insane, he found himself unwilling to break the contact. Without conscious thought he picked her up in his arms and carried her through the snow to the passenger side of the Explorer.

During their marriage he'd made certain they never experienced this kind of physical closeness, not even when they'd danced together at fund-raiser galas. Especially not then. Now he knew why.

For a year a fierce hunger had been burning inside him. A hunger he'd never dared feed, not when there couldn't be a future for the two of them.

Not when she would never love a man for the only reason that mattered.

The discovery that the woman he thought he'd said goodbye to forever had secretly followed him to Montana had all the components of some fantastic dream. But it was a flesh-and-blood Stefanie he deposited on the seat before removing her arms from his neck.

Determined to get this over as soon as possible, he stowed her purse and suitcase in his car, then started down the road.

She darted him an anxious glance. "Where are we going? The ranch is the other way."

"I'm taking you to Marion where there's a garage. The sooner your car is repaired, the sooner you can be on your way."

"No, Gabe!" Her body jerked toward him. "I—I mean, I need to talk to you. I had no idea the sheriff's office would send you to help me. Naturally I'm very grateful it was you who came." After a slight pause, "Now that you're here, couldn't we pull over to the side of the road for a minute?"

His hands tightened on the steering wheel. "It's getting late. We'll be lucky to catch the mechanic before he goes home for the night."

"I don't care about the car. This is more important."

With a grimace he asked, "You're not worried about where you're going to sleep tonight?"

"I was hoping I could stay with you," came the quiet response.

"That would be impossible."

Her head was bowed. "Is that because your son's mother wouldn't understand why your ex-wife has suddenly appeared, hoping to prevail on your good nature instead of partying in Paris?"

Gabe braked sharply, forgetting the snow. His Explorer skidded at an angle, but he was able to correct it in time to bring the car to a stop.

"All right, Stefanie. We're off the road. You've gotten your wish and have my undivided attention."

"Don't worry," she said quietly. "Your private life is your business. Rest assured your secret is safe with me. When the P.I.s saw you pick up a woman and a teenage boy who bore a resemblance to you, it wasn't hard to figure out th—"

"Get to the point!" he broke in, knocked sideways by her erroneous conclusions. "To say that I'm surprised to see you again would be the understatement of all time."

She nodded. "I know, but there are compelling reasons—at least compelling to me—why I was driven to follow you. If you'll just hear me out."

He sucked in his breath. "I'm listening."

"The truth is, I—I didn't want to go around the world alone. I realized you planned that trip as a fabulous thank-you gift for me. When you first suggested it, I felt it would have been unconscionable of me to turn it down. I could tell you were trying hard to do something special and unique for me. But as the days grew closer to my departure, I started to panic.''

A groan escaped his throat. ''Then why didn't you say something?''

''B-because I've never really been on my own before and knew it would be good for me. When you think about it, I've only lived with my parents, and then w-with you. Other people seem to handle independence just fine. But deep down the thought of being free to travel for six months by myself started to sound worse than being locked up in a prison.''

''For the love of heaven, Stefanie—'' He raked an unsteady hand through his hair. Her revelations were so unexpected, he wondered if there wasn't some other reason she'd come.

''Two days before you left Newport I got so frightened, I knew I would never be able to set foot on that plane to Paris. But I also knew you were depending on me to do my part and disappear.''

''Not at the cost of your sanity,'' he muttered fiercely.

''Gabe—I'm not trying to make you feel sorry for me. I'm just trying to explain that there was no way I would have let you down. S-so I came up with this plan to follow you, then beg you to let me stay wherever you were until the six months were up.''

He had to be dreaming. ''Why did you give the sheriff's office a fake name? For that matter, what are you doing in this disguise?''

''I didn't want anything I did to give your secret away. I knew how important it was for you to stay hidden from the media. To make certain no one recognized me or could link us in any way, I decided to camouflage myself and have been wearing this outfit since I left Newport.''

She'd come up with a good one. She was sexy as hell.

"At first I thought maybe you'd made arrangements to leave the States for good. Then came the surprising news that you were driving across the country. I had no idea you owned a ranch and planned to live out here."

"It's hardly the yacht club scene."

Her head jerked around. "I don't care about that, Gabe!"

Wouldn't it be amazing if her denial were true and she'd come after him because she couldn't help herself. But it was only in his dreams he heard her say those kinds of things to him…

"I haven't come here to cause you any trouble. I promise I haven't! The last thing I would want to do is interfere with your life."

"What am I supposed to say to that?" he let the sarcasm fly.

"I know my arrival has come as a horrible shock. But now that I'm here, maybe there's a job I could do? One of the P.I.s phoned the ranch and found out you run a school for troubled boys."

He let out an angry laugh. He couldn't help it.

"I don't know what it would be, of course," she offered lamely.

"Believe me, Stefanie, neither do I."

"The thing is, I would take on any task that would allow me to stay for six months and give me a roof over my head. With this disguise and my fake name, no one would ever need to know the truth of our relationship. I swear to you I would keep away from the people you love."

Gabe sat there in stunned silence. Gone was the composed, serene blond beauty he'd kissed goodbye on the cheek five days ago. In her place was this emotional, highly charged, intense woman in black curls who was talking faster and faster, a trait he'd never seen come out in her before.

"While I was waiting for help to arrive, I thought of an idea. Couldn't you tell your staff that I was driving to the ranch to apply for a position when my car got stuck? Of course, if that's totally unacceptable to you, would you mind if I tried to get a job in the area?"

She kneaded her hands together, another visible sign of her anxiety. "At least I would have the assurance that someone I once knew lived close by. I wouldn't feel so alone…"

The haunting tremor in her voice just now revealed a vulnerability Gabe would never have imagined was there. In the setting where she'd been raised, Stefanie had always appeared to be in charge. Confident. But that woman was no longer in evidence.

"Before you say no to everything, please be assured you have my word I won't retaliate by going home or revealing your secrets. It's just that I don't know where to turn."

A huge sigh escaped her lips.

"I realize everything's my fault. I should have told you I didn't want to go on that trip. But I was afraid to bother you when you were involved with your own plans. I'm so sorry, Gabe," she whispered shakily. "A-are you very angry?"

His dark head reared. *Hell, yes, he was angry.* And

frustrated. And tied up in so many knots he couldn't think straight. Her last words to him before he'd left the house kept resounding in his head.

You don't have to worry about me anymore. I took care of myself before we met, and shall do so again.

What was *that* all about? Which woman was the real Stefanie? Was it possible she'd come because she missed him? Or did she have some ulterior motive that would turn him inside out if he knew the answer?

Just then her stomach rumbled. Hadn't she been eating?

The sound brought him back to a cognizance of their surroundings. It had grown darker outside. Colder.

His first instinct was to send her to an opposite corner of the world. But he'd already tried that and it hadn't worked. She would have no choice if he decided to drive her to Marion and settle her in the Branding Iron for the night.

But when he considered she'd been on the road for the better part of a week, and had run into a ditch during the blizzard, he didn't like the idea of her spending another night alone in a tiny, sparsely furnished motel room way off the beaten track.

The coffee shop served as a local hangout for the cowboys in the area. On any given night things got a little wild in the bar. One look at Stefanie and...

Gabe started the engine and turned the Explorer around. In the semidarkness he felt her questioning gaze as if she'd touched him.

"It's late, Stafanie. You sound like you're ready to drop." He could tell she was exhausted. Even if nothing else added up, that much was true. "I'm taking you to the ranch."

"Thank you, Gabe," she murmured emotionally.

He didn't want her thanks. He didn't want her anywhere near him.

"You'd better reserve judgment. I'm afraid all the bedrooms in the main house are occupied by the school staff. But there's a small, semiempty room next to Marva's behind the kitchen that once served as a nursery."

"Who's Marva?"

"I hired her to be the cook, but she's also in charge of the main house."

"I see. Do *you* live in the main house?"

His jaw hardened. "Yes. Provided I can find a spare cot, you'll stay by her tonight and share her bathroom. Tomorrow morning will be soon enough to figure out what to do with you."

Her body shifted on the seat. "Please don't go to a lot of trouble for me. I don't take up much room and would be h-happy to sleep anywhere," she stammered.

He knew she wasn't being intentionally provocative, yet the word "anywhere" disturbed him. Under normal circumstances Gabe would offer her his king-size bed and take the couch downstairs in front of the fireplace. But the way he was feeling right now, he'd probably join her before morning without her permission.

To add to his guilt, she'd come begging to him like a homeless person in need of food and shelter. For all intents and purposes she *was* homeless, given the terms of their contract and his desire for both of them to remain out of touch with their old lives.

Six months.

He'd decreed it himself.

"Gabe?" She said his name hesitantly.

"What is it?"

He heard her pained little gasp before she said, "I know I'm a horrible inconvenience."

You've got that right.

"How do you want me to address you when we're not alone?"

After a year of marriage the question was so ludicrous, it went beyond the absurd.

"Like you would anyone else you'd just met."

More silence ensued, then, "Are you going to keep my identity a secret from everyone?"

With that searching question he flashed her an oblique glance. "If you're including Clay in your question, then yes. On the drive out from the East Coast, he mentioned that he'd seen a picture of you in the Newport paper. For the time being, it might be best if you stayed in disguise."

The troubled boys in his charge had been sent to this ranch to get away from worldly distractions. They, along with the staff, would do better not knowing that Gabe's beautiful socialite ex-wife was on the premises.

"Of course." Her head lowered. "He must be thrilled to have you around all the time. A boy needs his dad." Her voice shook.

"I agree. It's a shame Clay's father is dead."

CHAPTER THREE

STEFANIE was convinced she hadn't heard him right. "But I thoug—"

"You jumped to a wrong conclusion," he cut in on her. "Two years ago he got into serious drugs and did a lot of vandalizing. When the law caught up with him, his mother retained me. Since then I've been working with her to try to help him."

For two years Gabe had been seeing Clay's mother on a regular basis?

Any euphoria Stefanie had experienced over the news that he didn't have a son evaporated in light of that revelation.

"Does she live in Providence?"

"That's right. But I've arranged for her to fly out for regular visits."

Another dagger to her heart. "Why didn't she come all the way to the ranch this time?"

He sucked in his breath. "Because she wasn't feeling well."

"I see. Does she have other children?"

"No."

Stefanie stifled a moan. Now that Gabe was a divorced man, he didn't have to hide his relationship with the other woman who was closer to his age than Stefanie.

Naturally they'd been sleeping together from the outset. With Providence so close to Newport, it would explain his contentment while he'd been married to Stefanie.

The P.I. had said she was attractive.

Afraid one more question would give away her uncontrollable jealousy, Stefanie forced herself to look out the window and remain quiet for the rest of the drive to his ranch.

Clouds moved through the nighttime sky, obscuring the moon. Beyond the fences that lined the road, all she could make out were fields of snow and pines. The scene looked lonely and desolate.

More than ever she wondered why Gabe had turned his back on his former life. Something earth-shaking must have driven him to leave, but why come all the way out to this inhospitable place? How did he even find it?

No doubt he was hoping Clay's mother would like it. Even if she didn't, she would never let him know. No woman fortunate enough to be loved by Gabe would consider letting him go.

Was it her maturity and experience, her worldliness that had kept him interested all this time?

Stefanie had never slept with a man so she could hardly compete. By the time she'd reached the age where kissing boys helped her understand the meaning of physical desire, she'd met Gabe out sailing.

Of course he'd only looked upon her as one of the teenage girls in her flirtatious group of friends. But for Stefanie, those hours she spent as a guest on the Wainwright yacht had proved to be the defining moment of her life.

Surrounded by his brothers and extended family, Stefanie noted that he held himself somewhat aloof.

While everyone else played around, he appeared more serious and reflective.

Through covert glances she studied his bronzed, powerful physique, the way the wind tousled his black hair with its hint of curl. Just once she glimpsed the whiteness of his smile when he spotted some dolphins and pointed them out to her.

Though only a brief flash in time, they shared a private, wondrous moment. By the time it was over, she'd laid her heart at his feet.

Gabe personified manhood. As a result, no boy ever appealed to her again.

After thanking him personally for the wonderful day, she left the yacht with an indelible memory of black-fringed eyes, green as the ocean swells. By the time she waved to him from the deck of her family's sailboat, she'd made up her mind that when she grew up, she was going to marry him.

An expert sailor herself, she set a steady course toward him with all the genius of the Admiral of the Fleet.

Her best friend, Louise, told her she was crazy.

Honestly, Steffie, by the time you reach the age where a gorgeous male like Gabriel Wainwright will bother to look at you as a woman, he'll be a senator himself, married to someone else equally gorgeous and they'll probably have several children. Give it up!

But Stefanie ignored her friend's advice. Gabe was the crème de la crème. After high school came university where she received a degree in economics, her father's passion.

Wanting some hands-on experience after four years of theory, her mother suggested she apply for a fund-raising job. Why not go to work for Senator Wainwright's reelection campaign?

The idea appealed for several reasons one of which was that it would throw her in Gabriel Wainwright's arena. He was still Rhode Island's most eligible bachelor.

In time she became good friends with the senator and his wife. More and more their families mingled on a social as well as political level. She began to see Gabe coming and going.

They would smile. Sometimes he would stop to discuss an aspect of his father's campaign with her before talking to someone else. She always kept things friendly and upbeat, never allowing him a glimpse of the torrid storm of desire raging inside her.

Then came the kind of day she'd been praying for. The senator wanted to run a speech by his youngest son before he spoke at an important press conference on the environment. Unfortunately no one could locate Gabe. Since the senator was set to go on the air at 8:30 p.m., that left a small window of three hours in which to find him.

Stefanie, along with other staff people, volunteered to look for him. Armed with a copy of the speech, she rushed home. Obeying a hunch, she took out her dad's launch and headed for an area near the Wainwright estate where she knew he often sailed after being in court all day.

It was a slightly chilly afternoon. When she couldn't see his sailboat, she got out the binoculars. All she spotted was a small fishing trawler pulled up to shore where someone had made a fire. Upon closer investigation she discovered it was Gabe.

He was by himself, cleaning fish.

Not at any time since she'd first met him had she ever found herself alone with him.

She made her approach and cut the motor, but her heart was hammering so hard, she was afraid he would hear it. As the launch slid to a stop on the sand, Gabe got up from his haunches to assist her.

Before she jumped to shore, there was that split second when she encountered a look of such sensual male appraisal, her bones turned to liquid. It was the look she'd been waiting years to evoke.

She'd proved Louise wrong. He wasn't a senator yet, nor was he married with a couple of children...

"Your father's been looking for you. He'd like you to go over this before the press conference tonight." She held out the envelope containing his speech, but Gabe didn't take it.

His eyes narrowed on her upturned face. She could no longer read their expression. "My father's very fortunate to have someone as loyal and devoted to him as you are. I hope he tells you that on occasion."

Gabe's unexpected remarks baffled her. They weren't a criticism exactly, but for some odd reason she sensed his displeasure. Whether of her or his father, or both, she couldn't tell.

"Would you like me to open the envelope and read it to you?"

"No."

She swallowed hard at the terse reply.

"Shall I leave it then?"

"No," he said again.

The tension coming from him was palpable. Stefanie stared into the dying flames. Something else was on his mind. She prayed it had to do with her. Something personal and intimate.

Seconds passed. She waited to hear him ask her to stay with him. When the words didn't come she finally said, "Your father needs feedback before he goes on the air at eight-thirty."

After a debilitating silence he murmured, "I wonder if you would be as faithful to me if *I* asked you a favor."

The brooding side of his nature was in full evidence. She darted him another questioning glance. "I don't understand."

"Would you dare return to my father and admit you couldn't find me?"

If this was some kind of a test, she knew exactly where her loyalty lay. Where it had always lain. Only then did she realize she'd intruded on a very private moment. It was possible she'd committed the unpardonable. If that was true, then her dreams had been in vain.

Feeling desolate, she started for the launch. "I never saw you," she called over her shoulder before pushing off.

Though he made no answering comment, he helped steady her boat against the incoming surf. Thigh deep in the water, he remained there until she started the motor and took off.

Three weeks later came the call from out of the blue. It was Gabe asking her to dinner. By the time he'd brought her home, she'd agreed to become his wife. *But never his lover.*

"Stefanie?"

The deep male voice she loved so well jerked her back to the present. "Yes?" she whispered.

"Are you all right? Did you hurt yourself when your car went into the ditch?"

"I—I wasn't injured, but I can feel a headache coming on."

"You need food. We're almost home."

He said the word "home" so easily. Why not? He'd been coming here for well over a year. To him, the house in Newport complete with cardboard wife had represented little more than a luxury hotel with maid service between romantic stopovers to Providence.

Stefanie had no right to feel betrayed or jealous, but those emotions were there just the same, embittering her to the point she didn't like herself anymore.

She was so tired of the struggle. She loved him so terribly.

What would she do if he told her she had to leave as soon as her car was ready?

What would she do?

The Explorer pulled to a stop near a medium-size ranch house whose roof was hidden under a layer of snow. There were other buildings in the periphery, but in the dark it was difficult to make them out.

"Let's get you inside."

She seemed to be moving in slow motion. Before she could open the door, Gabe had come around to her side of the car to help her out. It felt wonderful to be under his protection again.

On their way to the house he cupped her elbow to steady her footsteps through the slush. She could hear barking inside. Soon a petite, middle-aged woman with light brown hair appeared in the doorway.

"Marva?" he called to her. "We've got a visitor for the night."

"Clover figured that out before I did." At the mention of its name, a large collie rushed past the cook to greet Gabe in delight. Soon it was running circles around Stefanie, sniffing at her hands.

The woman chuckled. "You must be Teri. Welcome to the Larch Tree Ranch. I'm glad to see you're all right."

"Thank you, Marva. Believe me, I'm very grateful to be here in one piece."

"Let's hope the car Ms. Jones was driving fared as well," Gabe muttered in a dry tone. He started to usher her inside, but Stefanie held back.

When she looked up, he was staring into her eyes. "Don't be nervous of Clover. Pat her head and she'll know you're a friend."

Stefanie wasn't frightened of the dog. She'd grown up in a loving home with several dogs and had adored them.

If her marriage to Gabe had been normal, she would have talked to him about getting one. But since he was never home except to sleep, and had never brought up the subject, she'd decided he didn't want an animal around, fearing he didn't like them. Clover's presence put that concern to rest.

No. Stefanie's hesitation had more to do with Gabe calling her *Ms. Jones*. It made this charade far too real. They were both playing a role in a ghastly variation of an old game started a long time ago. She hated it! Beneath the surface she knew Gabe was impatiently counting the hours until he could send her on her way in the morning.

Like a restive child waiting to be recognized,

Clover made several moaning sounds. Stefanie quickly averted her eyes from Gabe's and reached out to scratch the dog's head.

"With those intelligent eyes, you're a real beauty, aren't you girl," she murmured, running a hand along the collie's back to her tail.

"It looks like you've made a friend for life," Marva observed. "When you're ready, I've got lamb stew and corn bread waiting for you."

Suddenly Gabe wheeled away from Stefanie. "Hold my dinner, Marva. Before it gets any later, I'm going to pull that car out of the ditch. Then I'll find a cot for Ms. Jones. She can sleep in the nursery tonight."

Stefanie would have felt abandoned except for the dog who looked back at her with pleading eyes, apparently waiting for her to join Gabe.

"Clover!"

The dog bounded off, obeying her master's voice. A little shiver chased across Stefanie's skin. She hurried into the house.

"There's a guest bathroom behind the stairs where you can freshen up first. Follow me." If Marva had felt the tension just now, she didn't show any sign of it.

The old ranch house was a rustic affair built entirely of logs. Laid out in a simple design, various rooms led off from a central hallway. On her left Stefanie noted an office. To her right was a small, cozy-looking living room with a stone fireplace at one end.

Past the stairs with half-sawn logs serving for steps, she found the bathroom. Beyond it she spied a pair of double doors with mullioned glass leading to a large dining room cum kitchen. This part of the house came as a surprise with its vaulted ceiling and wall of windows laid out in a geometric design, reminding her of a modern cathedral.

Obviously this portion had been remodeled to accommodate more bodies. Cheerful red plaid oilcloths covered six round tables with captain's chairs. She could imagine a bunch of starving boys anxious to congregate for meals in here.

Already Stefanie knew this was her favorite room. No doubt it was everyone's who lived and worked at the ranch. She suspected this was all Gabe's doing. *His* genius.

A pain as real as if she'd been stabbed passed through her heart to realize she'd known so little about him. For their entire marriage he'd kept this secret to himself.

Since he'd trusted her enough to draw up that hateful contract in the first place, why hadn't he talked to her about his plans? Didn't he know she would have loved to share in his ideas? Help him?

No matter if he was in love with someone else, did she seem so shallow, so incapable of making a contribution to a cause that had nothing to do with his father's politics, she hadn't even registered on his consciousness?

Feeling like the walking wounded, she availed herself of the rest room, then joined Marva who'd set a place for her at one of the tables in the dining room.

Once again guilt racked Stefanie. Because of her accident, Gabe had been forced to come to her rescue, causing him to miss his dinner.

If there was one thing she *did* know about her ex-husband, he had a healthy appetite. They'd been to enough public functions together for her to testify to that fact. After being married to him, she was an expert on his public persona.

It was his private life that had always eluded her...

Gabe wasn't just a good man. She'd known from the beginning he was destined to become a great man. Everyone who'd ever rubbed shoulders with him knew it.

Not in her wildest dreams would she have imagined him turning down his birthright to live out the rest of his life in this back of beyond.

To be entrenched in a lifestyle so foreign to his upbringing meant the seeds for total change must have been planted in his soul years ago. Maybe as early as his teens when she would have been a mere toddler.

If only he would give her the chance, Stefanie yearned to talk to him about it. She ached to hear whatever he was willing to tell her about a decision that was going to rock his family's world when it finally came out.

"More stew, Teri?"

"Oh—no, thank you, Marva. It was so delicious I've already had two helpings of everything. Now I'm full."

"How about another cup of tea?"

"I couldn't."

She cleared her dishes and took them over to the sink, but Marva prevented her from rinsing them off.

"Mr. Wainwright wouldn't approve of a guest working in the kitchen."

"That's nonsense." Stefanie stood her ground, refusing to move out of the way. "He's pulling my car from the ditch, and you've had to warm up a meal for me at the last minute. This is the least I can do to repay you.''

Marva shook her head. ''He's not going to like it.''

''What aren't I going to like?''

Both women turned their heads in time to see Gabe's masculine frame enter the back door. He pulled a roll-away bed after him. It was already made up with sheets and a blanket, but Stefanie scarcely noticed. She was too busy feasting her eyes on Gabe.

He'd always looked wonderful in a tux or an expensive silk suit. But the well-worn Stetson and jacket combined with blue jeans molding his powerful thighs, brought out his stunning virility in a way that left her breathless.

''Teri's determined to earn her keep!'' Marva replied by way of explanation.

Stefanie couldn't see Gabe's expression because it was partially hidden by his cowboy hat. But she figured she was damned in his eyes no matter what she did or didn't do.

Thankfully the collie had no reservations. It warmed Stefanie's heart when she squeezed past Gabe and darted toward Stefanie, rubbing her head against her legs.

''Marva? While I bring in her bags from the car, why don't you show Ms. Jones where she'll be sleeping tonight?''

His use of the word ''tonight'' sounded ominous to Stefanie whose spirits took another dive. As for the cook, she didn't look pleased with his suggestion.

''What about your dinner?''

''I'll fix myself something later, so don't worry about it. Come on, Clover.''

This time the dog obeyed Gabe without question, having learned her lesson about hanging around Stefanie too long the first time.

The second they disappeared into the night, Stefanie walked over to the cot and started pushing it toward the double doors she'd entered earlier. Again she had the impression Marva wasn't at all happy about the situation.

Stefanie couldn't tell if the older woman was upset because this was her domain and her routine had been interrupted, or because she considered Stefanie's presence an invasion of her privacy.

The last thing Stefanie wanted was to become Marva's enemy.

They went through the French doors to the back hallway of the original part of the cabin. Marva indicated the bathroom on the right, then came to a standstill at the first doorway on the left. A frown marred her features.

"This is it," she muttered. "Mr. Wainwright calls it the nursery because of the small set of dresser drawers and white crib folded up against the log wall. There's no window or overhead light. No rug to cover the pine flooring. The only thing I can tell you is that it's clean because a crew drove up from Kalispell last week to do the Spring housecleaning."

"This will be wonderful!" Stefanie rushed to assure her.

"There's no heating vent."

"Don't worry."

She pushed the cot all the way inside, then undid the catch. When the ends of the bed opened to the floor, it filled the empty space. But Stefanie didn't care about it being wall-to-wall bed. She would willingly undergo any deprivation, including a cold room. Now that she'd found Gabe, nothing else mattered except that she be allowed to stay with him.

"I'll put out a set of yellow towels in the bathroom for you. Is there anything else you need?"

"Nothing else. You've been so kind. Thank you, Marva."

"You're welcome. I hope you get a good sleep. See you in the morning." She hurried off.

While Stefanie was puffing up the pillow, she heard footsteps in the hall. Gabe had to be coming. Stefanie could tell by the sound of his boots against the wood flooring.

He paused at the doorway, blotting out most of the light. Like a silhouette, she could see the outline of his powerful frame. Her heart leaped to her throat.

"I—I'm sorry you had to pull my car from the ditch. Is it badly damaged?"

"Except for a few dents to the front bumper, it's in relatively good shape. Where would you like your bags?"

"Just l-leave them in the hall against the wall." She was already breathless.

He put them down. Before she could countenance it, he moved inside and shut the door, enclosing them in total darkness. If she reached out, she would be able to touch him.

"How did you come by a pair of Arizona license plates with a current registration?" His low, deep voice permeated her insides.

The question was so unexpected, it caught her off guard.

"I didn't steal them, if that's what you mean."

"Did I imply that you did?" he asked silkily.

"No—" she blurted nervously. "Of course not. It's just that knowing your father would try to find m...us when he learned we'd gone away—"

Dear God, if Gabe ever discovered the truth about what she'd told their parents that evening at the Newport Yacht Club...

"I paid the P.I.s extra money to do what they had to do to make certain he couldn't trace me. In case you're harboring any fears in that department, let me assure you I used cash to buy the car in Sterling."

"You mean Connecticut?" He sounded incredulous.

"Yes."

"*When?*"

"As soon as you left for the airport in the limo, one of the P.I.s from the firm I'd contacted drove me there to get it. Later, after I started on my trip across the country, I paid cash for gas and food and motels. Whenever I had to register at the desk, I listed my home address as Flagstaff, Arizona."

Though it was black as night in the small enclosure, she could feel the tension emanating from him. "Did you cancel your tour?"

"No," her voice trembled. "I was afraid to do anything that would make your father suspicious. The thing is, I know it cost you a great deal of money. That's what I wanted to talk to you about.

"I—If you would let me work here for you, there would be no reason to pay me a wage. Anything I earn could go toward the money I owe you for the tour. It will probably take me years, but I promise I'll pay you back every cent."

"Forget the money. It's the least of my concerns," came the grating response.

Stefanie shuddered because she could tell he was barely suppressing his anger.

"I realize that. You're afraid your father will pick up on my trail. But I was so careful. I don't see how he could possi—"

"On this ranch, everyone goes to bed early," he broke in coldly, as if she hadn't spoken. "That includes unexpected visitors. If you want breakfast before you leave in the morning, report to the kitchen at seven."

She couldn't prevent the gasp that escaped. "You mean you won't consider hiring me?"

"It means there's no opening." His calm reply maddened her.

Desperate at this point she cried out, "Not even for an extra cowhand?"

An unsettling silence ensued.

"The Stefanie Dawson I know is one of the best political party-givers and fund-raisers on the planet. But unless I've missed something, she hasn't been on a horse since her one and only pony ride on her eighth birthday."

Though he'd only spoken the truth, his mockery stung.

"I could learn, Gabe."

"To ride a horse, perhaps. A cowhand is something else again. That's my foreman's department. Good night."

"Wait—"

She heard his sharp intake of breath. He'd reached the end of his patience, but she was fighting for his love!

"If your foreman were willing to train me, would you let me stay?"

"It would never happen so it's a moot point. Sleep well. You'll need it for the drive ahead of you tomorrow."

On that chilling note he exited the miniscule room, leaving the door slightly ajar.

Stefanie waited until she could no longer hear the tread of his cowboy boots. Then she darted out of the room toward the door at the end of the hall.

Tapping against the varnished wood, she called out Marva's name. The older woman appeared a minute later dressed in a nightgown and robe.

"Yes, Teri?"

"Please forgive me for disturbing you, but I need some information before you go to sleep. I came to the ranch looking for a job. Mr. Wainwright said his foreman was the man to approach about it. I'd like to talk to him as soon as possible. Maybe at breakfast?"

Marva's eyes widened. "*You* want an outdoor job?" She sounded shocked.

"Yes. I—I need the work."

The older woman blinked. "Well, if that's what Gabe said, your best time to catch Mack is around five-thirty in the morning. He'll be in the barn saddling up for work with the other hands. The men don't come in to breakfast until eight, after the boys have been fed."

"I see. Where is the barn?"

"Didn't Gabe tell you?"

Stefanie averted her eyes. "I—I'm sure he would have if something more important hadn't come up requiring his presence." Another white lie, but it couldn't be helped.

"That something usually has to do with one of our

boarders," Marva muttered. "He's a father figure to all of them. My land, those boys don't know how lucky they are." She sighed. "Oh—just listen to me babble on when you were asking about the barn! Follow the road behind the main ranch house for a quarter of a mile. It'll be on your left."

Hungry for any information about Gabe's life here in Montana, Stefanie was dying to ask more questions. But she didn't dare. The cook might become more suspicious than she already was over Stefanie's desire to work as a stockwoman.

"Thanks for your help, Marva. I promise not to disturb you again."

"Don't worry about it. After you've had your interview, come on back for breakfast."

"I will."

On the way to her room, Stefanie made a detour to the bathroom with her luggage. After putting out a fresh change of jeans and a sweater, she got ready for bed and set her windup alarm clock for five.

Because she couldn't lock her door, she had to sleep with her wig on. The contact lenses were a different story. She took them out and put them in the case with the solution at the side of the roll-away bed. The other case she kept in the glove compartment of the car.

The cot mattress felt soft and was probably bad for a person's back, but she was so thankful to be sleeping under the same roof as Gabe, nothing else mattered.

Tomorrow morning she had a job to do. Instead of charming a wealthy business magnate into giving a generous donation for the Wainwright war chest, she would charm Gabe's foreman into giving her a job, even if it meant he had to create one for her.

The only foremen who came to mind were those she'd seen depicted in vintage Western movies. Hard-bitten loner types who preferred men's company except on the weekend when they visited the local saloon for cards, whiskey and a little female company. Perhaps the stereotype had been exaggerated for the screen, but Stefanie had an idea today's foreman wasn't that much different from sixty years ago.

If she were to come across as the wealthy, sophisticated, liberated, savvy twenty-first century female she'd been raised to be, she probably wouldn't get to first base.

Gabe knew that, which was why he'd discounted her idea out of hand. But not even he understood how determined she was to stay on the ranch.

Since she knew nothing about horses, her instincts told her she'd have much better luck with this Mack if she acted submissive, helpless, yet willing to learn. A few tears of gratitude and some compliments for his manliness might help to accomplish what Gabe had declared impossible.

CHAPTER FOUR

"CLOVER? Quiet down."

The dog stopped moaning but she continued to pace Gabe's bedroom until he threw back the covers in frustration.

"We've already been out twice. What's gotten into you?"

Normally she curled up on the rug by the side of his bed. Tonight instead, she was acting as nervy as an expectant mother about to give birth to her first litter.

When she made another strange sound in her throat, Gabe turned on the bedside lamp.

"What in the devil?"

The dog was carrying his sweater in her mouth. She must have pulled it off the chair where he'd left it.

"Come here, girl. Give it to me."

With reluctance, Clover dropped it by the side of the bed. Gabe picked it up. It was the navy crew neck he'd been wearing all day. The one he'd had on when he'd pulled Stefanie from the car earlier that evening.

Suddenly illumination dawned.

Clover had a hunter's instinct and could smell Stefanie's scent on the wool. Now that Gabe thought about it, the dog had been unexpectedly familiar with Stefanie from the moment he'd met her.

Gabe hadn't been able to account for it, but now he was remembering other moments in the past when the dog had sniffed at his clothing after a flight from Rhode Island. Maybe it was the scent from their Newport home he'd brought with him, a scent the dog recognized when Stefanie had patted her.

With that thought, another vivid memory assailed him. One of Stefanie getting down on a level with his dog to examine her in the same easy manner a true dog lover would behave.

Her spontaneous action didn't mesh with something Mrs. Dawson had confided to him about her daughter not being able to tolerate dogs.

Early into their marriage, Gabe had wanted to make Stefanie a gift of one to keep her company when he was out of town. But after her mother's remark, Gabe had abandoned the idea, especially when Stefanie had never expressed the desire for a pet.

He leaned over and rubbed the dog's head in his hands. "I know you want to go downstairs and get better acquainted with her, but you can't. She's asleep, and tomorrow she'll be leaving, so there's no point. Be a good girl and lie down."

After she did his bidding, he tossed the sweater to the chair in the far corner, then turned out the light. An hour later he was still lying against the pillows with his hands behind his head, wide-awake.

There was no way in hell he would ever have peace of mind if he let Stefanie stay on the ranch. Her presence had turned his world inside out. The memory of the feel of her body was a continual torment.

Gabe was no masochist. His only course of action was to get rid of her tomorrow.

She'd mentioned working somewhere in the area.

He supposed she could go to Kalispell. A couple of phone calls to several acquaintances and he could probably arrange a temporary job for her. Something low-profile. With her expertise both at raising and keeping track of campaign funds, she was a whiz on the computer.

Kalispell was far enough away that he wouldn't have to see her unless there was an emergency of some kind. New apartments had sprung up. Some were furnished. He would make certain she had tight security.

But no matter how many scenarios he thought up for her, in the end he came to the conclusion that it was pointless. Stefanie's decision not to go on that world tour had changed all the rules.

It still puzzled him that she hadn't flown to Paris at least. If she was truly as frightened to be alone as she'd said, she obviously needed to be back in Newport, living in the house he'd given her where she felt safe.

He'd already robbed her of a year and a half of her life if he counted their engagement period. After all she'd done for him, she had every right to get back to her world as soon as possible. The man destiny had handpicked for her was waiting somewhere out there…

The sooner she met him, the sooner she could start to make her own dreams come true.

Gabe must have been out of his mind to expect her to go abroad for half a year. Too caught up in his own selfish plans, he'd sent her off like a good little soldier, never seeing through that brave façade of hers.

It was time he faced reality.

What did it matter when his father learned the truth of everything? Tomorrow or six months from now, the result would be the same. The inevitable confrontation Gabe had been dreading would take place.

At least when the final break came, he would be able to take solace in the fact that his dream for a boys' ranch was already a fait accompli.

A feat he couldn't have accomplished without Stefanie.

With his mind made up to drive her to the airport in the morning, Gabe turned on his stomach, willing sleep to obliterate the pain.

To his chagrin, he wrestled demons for the rest of the night. When he couldn't handle them any longer, he got up and took a cold shower.

Clover stood at the door, impatiently swishing her tail while he dressed.

"I know why you're so excited," Gabe muttered, already experiencing a yawning emptiness because after this morning Stefanie would no longer be here. *Not ever again.*

After putting on his boots, he opened the door to his bedroom. "Let's go, girl."

But his words were wasted on Clover who leaped ahead of him in pursuit of his prey, which happened to be a particularly breathtaking human being.

By the time Gabe reached the downstairs foyer, the dog had made the rounds of the ranch house and now stood at the front door barking. No doubt Stefanie was still asleep and would probably stay that way for some time.

Gabe checked his watch. It was quarter to six. Clover needed to go out. As he opened the door for her, he noticed that Stefanie's blue Honda wasn't standing next to the Explorer where he'd parked it last night.

Had he been so cruel to her, she'd left to avoid having to face him again?

Feeling as if someone had kicked him in the gut, he hurried outside to a chilly morning. The snow revealed Clover's paw prints, but the predawn sky made it difficult to see details further away.

His dog ran ahead of him. Upon reaching the corner of the ranch house, she stopped and barked. When Gabe realized the intelligent animal was following a set of tire tracks belonging to Stefanie's car, he praised Clover and took off after her.

To his relief, the tracks led around the back of the house. The barn and bunkhouse were the only other buildings set away from the main cluster, but they lay around a curve in the road, a quarter of a mile from view. Had Stefanie gone exploring, or was she lost?

If her intention had been to leave the property, thank heaven she hadn't found her way out yet. Much as he wanted her gone from his life, he needed to know she was safe.

The interior of the barn could only be a few degrees above freezing. The lucky horses had been born with hairy coats. Stefanie had to make do with her parka, which she'd zipped to the chin.

Most of the horses stared at her through the openings in the slats while they calmly munched on hay. She stopped at the farthest stall to admire the handsome chestnut. He was huge. When she spoke to him, he backed away.

"Don't be scared of me," she said in a gentle voice, wondering at the horse's reaction when she must look so puny to him. But she was the intruder after all.

"Caesar hasn't been formally introduced. That's why he seems offish," a pleasant male voice spoke behind her.

"Oh!" Stefanie whirled around in embarrassment. "I didn't hear anyone enter the barn."

A lean man she figured to be around forty with light brown hair and warm brown eyes stood there appraising her. He was of average height and very nice looking. Probably one of the hands.

"My name is Teri Jones. I've been waiting to talk to the foreman. Marva told me I might find him in here at this hour."

A smile lit up his face, making him appear younger. "She was right. I'm Mack Whittaker." He put out his hand, which she shook. "How can I help you?"

It seemed the old stereotype foreman portrayed in the Western films had done her a great disservice. She doubted her plan to go all helpless on Gabe's right hand man would work.

Whatever she said or did now would determine whether she stayed on the ranch or not. Maybe honesty was the best approach. Enough honesty without giving everything away.

She took a deep breath. "I came to the ranch looking for a job. I've never been on a horse, let alone worked around them. But I'm willing to learn. I-it's *vital* that I learn," her voice trembled.

"Please, Mr. Whittaker— If you'll just give me a

chance, I'll prove to you I'm a hard worker. I'll do any task!

"The thing is, Mr. Wainwright knows how busy you are and didn't suppose you had the time or inclination to take me on, even if you needed help. In fact h-he doesn't know I came on my own to talk to you, so please don't blame him. This was all my idea."

He shoved his cowboy hat further back on his head. "Mind if I ask why you want ranch work when it's so foreign to you?"

Relieved he hadn't yet told her she was wasting her time she blurted, "Not at all— You see, I need to prove to myself that I can do something entirely different than I'm used to doing."

By now his eyes were smiling. "And what is that?"

"You might say I've been a girl Friday." In a way, it was the truth. He just didn't know *where* she'd been a glorified dogsbody, or from whom she'd taken her orders.

"But it's not enough. I need to find out who I really am, how tough I really am. Can you understand that, Mr. Whittaker?"

His gaze played over her features. "The name is Mack. I believe I do understand. However, it's hard to learn this business if you haven't grown up around it."

"But not impossible, surely!"

"That all depends on the person."

"Would you be willing to take me on probation? I swear you won't be sorry."

His eyes squinted. "You say you've never been on a horse?"

"Only a pony, when I was a little girl."

"Where was that?"

She swallowed hard. This was the part she hated, having to tell him a lie. "Flagstaff, Arizona. Please, Mack. Just pretend I'm a man. What's the first thing you would tell me to do?"

"Muck out the stalls."

"You mean get rid of the manure."

"That's right." He chuckled. "And spread fresh straw around."

"While the horses are still in there?"

Her question provoked a belly laugh. "No."

He would never hire her. She'd lost her last chance. The thought of having to leave Gabe was so painful, tears filled her eyes before she could hide them.

"Hey—" He frowned. "I didn't mean to make you cry."

"You didn't. It's just that I wanted a job here so badly. Yet even *I* can see I'm the last person anyone would think of hiring. Forgive me for taking up your time."

"Hang on there—" He called her back as she headed for the door. "You may not know anything about horses, but it's obvious you came to me in all sincerity. I tell you what."

With those four words, her heart rate started to accelerate.

"If you're going to work for me, you need to buy yourself some clothes you won't be afraid to get dirty. While you're at it, might as well throw in a pair of cowboy boots and warm gloves.

"Starting tomorrow morning at seven, you'll spend time in here with the students getting used to being around the horses. Everyone's learning how to feed them and keep the place clean.

"Each day after lunch, I'll teach you how to ride. After two weeks I'll make my decision whether to put you on the payroll permanently."

Two weeks to be near Gabe.

The thought filled her with such intense joy, she wanted to throw her arms around the foreman's neck. Instead she had to fight to restrain herself.

"Thank you, Mack. You don't know what this means to me," she murmured emotionally. "I'll work so hard, you'll never regret giving me this opportunity. Oh, I forgot to ask. Where do the hands sleep?"

"We have our own bunkhouse."

"Is there room for one more?"

A ruddy color crept into his cheeks. It told her a lot about the mild mannered foreman. He was a hardworking cowboy who happened to be a gentleman. She imagined the combination was a rarity. Gabe had known what he was doing when he'd hired him to work around other people's troubled sons.

"Don't worry about it, Mack. I'll find my own lodgings. See you at seven."

She hurried out the door, anxious to drive to Kalispell for some serious shopping. In her eagerness to reach the car, she didn't see the blur of brown and white fur until Gabe's dog circled her legs, causing her to tip facedown in the snow.

"Clover!" A burst of laughter escaped her lips as the friendly collie began licking her face. They rolled around in the snow playing together for a few minutes.

When she turned on her back, it was a taut-faced

Gabe she could see running toward her in thigh-molding jeans and a plaid flannel shirt. In the next instant he'd helped her to her feet.

Against a lavender sky, the black of his hair and searching green eyes leaped out at her, causing her to marvel all over again at his distinct male beauty.

"Are you all right?"

The deep timbre revealed he hadn't been up very long. Maybe it was because he was winded that she thought his voice sounded anxious.

In her excitement to find herself alone with him, she was a little slow on the uptake. "I'm f-fine," she rushed to reassure him. "We're fine, aren't we, Clover!" She reached for the dog like a lifeline so Gabe wouldn't guess how his mere touch could melt her insides to liquid.

"What were you doing back here?"

She'd been waiting for that question with a certain amount of dread. When she raised her head to face him once more, only then did she notice he wasn't wearing a coat. He must have left the ranch house in a big hurry.

"I wanted to talk to your foreman. Marva indicated I might find him in the barn if I got up early enough."

Gabe's jaw hardened, causing perspiration to break out on her hairline. "And did you?" he ground out.

Growing increasingly nervous, she moistened her lips. "Yes."

His expression looked like thunder. "With what result?"

"H-he's going to let me apprentice for two

weeks," she stammered. "If I pass the test, then he'll let me stay on."

An ominous silence followed.

Then he asked, "Doing what?"

"Mucking out the stalls."

His head reared back while he muttered something she'd never heard come out of his mouth before.

Stung by his reaction she said, "Mack obviously has a lot more faith in my abilities than you do."

A wintry smile broke out on Gabe's face. His gaze made a bold assessment of her features and body, not missing a single line or curve along the way. "It wasn't his faith in your abilities that got *you* hired, sweetheart."

Gabe was angry. Angrier than she'd ever seen him. But for an infinitesimal moment she'd glimpsed the banked fire in his eyes as they'd swept over her.

Suddenly she was transported back to the time she'd gone searching for him in her father's launch. When she'd found him, those green depths had sent out that same unmistakable glint of male desire at its most elemental level, thrilling her to the very core of her being.

No matter how furious he was, she had proof that he wasn't totally indifferent to her physical presence.

Taking a calculated risk she said, "Since you have such grave misgivings where I'm concerned, I'll save you the trouble of telling him he made a mistake in hiring me."

On a burst of inspiration she sank her hand into the dog's fur. "Come on, Clover. You can help me resign." Without waiting for Gabe's reaction, she started for the barn door.

Bless Clover's heart, she stuck to Stefanie's side

like a new foal with her mother. Within inches of pulling on the handle, Stefanie felt a hand of steel on her arm before she was spun around.

As if she were so much fluff, Gabe practically dragged her away from the entrance. His mouth had thinned to a white line of fury. This time a thrill of fear darted through her body.

"You're not going in there and quit the job he just offered you!" he said in an icy tone, his hands still gripping her upper arms. "Mack will want to know the reason why. When you tell him it's because I don't approve, he'll think I don't have confidence in him.

"Once trust is gone, he'll leave, destroying the community I've spent the last year developing here. Hiring a good foreman is difficult at best. To find someone with Mack's qualities is something of a miracle."

Gabe's rebuke would have hurt at any time. But it was the passion behind the words that made her realize she didn't dare trifle with this world he'd embraced heart and soul. She didn't have the right! Because of her own selfish needs, she'd put him in a terrible position.

It had been wrong of her to follow him to Montana. Totally and utterly wrong.

"I have no desire to undermine you, Gabe," she whispered. "Mack's given me two weeks. When the time is up, I'll thank him for taking a chance on me. Then I'll tell him I'm going back to Flagstaff where I belong.

"Now, if you'll let go of me, I have some errands to run."

Her words must have jolted him back to an awareness of what he was doing. In the next breath she was free of his firm grasp, the last thing she wanted.

"What errands?" The terseness of his question left another wound that wouldn't heal.

"I need appropriate clothes to wear when I start my job in the morning. A-and there's the matter of a place to stay. I should imagine the Branding Iron will let me make a short-term arrangemen—"

"The motel is out!" he cut in brutally. "For security reasons as well as practicality, everyone lives on the ranch. After the lifestyle you're used to, I realize the old nursery hardly passes for a bedroom. But it's exactly where you'll be spending your nights until you leave."

She turned away from him, afraid he'd see the happiness in her eyes. *If only you knew, my darling, that I'm just happy to be near you.*

Cupping her elbow in an impersonal manner he said, "I'll drive you back to the house, then we'll take the Explorer into Kalispell."

If she understood him correctly, he was going to take her shopping. She could scarcely contain her excitement as she got in the passenger seat. But it was short-lived when he added, "Clay can come with us. I promised his mother to outfit him as soon as we arrived."

On that note he shut her door and walked around to the driver's side of the car. She derived pleasure from just watching him. He adjusted the seat for his long hard-muscled legs before getting behind the wheel.

"What about Clover?"

"She can follow us."

The collie had run around to Stefanie's side of the car again.

"But she wants to be with us. Look at her face, those sad eyes. She's not even wagging her tail."

Another unintelligible epithet escaped Gabe's lips. "She'll live." He turned on the engine and backed the car around.

"It's obvious she adores you. How long have you had her?"

"After I bought the ranch, I made several visits to the pound looking for a trained animal that would make a good watchdog. I eventually brought Clover home with me."

"She's beautiful! How did she end up in there?"

"The first time I saw her, she was near death. Whoever the owner was had abandoned her. She needed a lot of help. The vet for the ranch didn't think she would make it without constant nursing care. I decided she'd be a good project for the boys."

Her eyes misted over imagining the love Clover must feel for Gabe because of his compassion and gentle care.

Throughout their short-lived marriage, Stefanie had worshipped the remarkable man sitting on the other side of the car from her, but he'd always kept her at a distance, never allowing her to see beneath the surface.

Since her arrival at the ranch, something miraculous had happened. Despite all his efforts to push her away, she'd been given a glimpse into his psyche— the core part of him that made him tick.

Though she didn't know the underlying motive for his turning to this life, she recognized that he must have undergone an earthshaking experience. But there was one thing she'd already come to understand. Gabe's goals were unique. He was another breed of man. *How she loved him!*

"Stefanie?"

She jerked her head around, surprised to discover they'd reached the front of the ranch house. "Yes?"

"Did you eat breakfast before you left for the barn?"

She shook her head.

He started to get out of the car. "I'm going inside to find Clay. Do what you need to do, then meet us back at the Explorer in ten minutes. We'll grab a bite to eat in town."

Normally Gabe helped her from the car. Not *this* morning. After calling to Clover who wasn't far behind, they disappeared into the house before she'd had time to swing her feet to the ground.

By now the sun had come up over the horizon. The storm had blown itself out. Already the air was much warmer. It was going to be a beautiful day. She spied patches of ground where the snow was melting. Water dripped from the eaves.

After the long, dark winter, there were definite signs of spring in Montana. Now that things had worked out for her to be around Gabe a little longer, she could feel them in her heart. Very ephemeral, but there all the same, pulsating with life.

This time when she entered the house, she could hear voices coming from the dining room. Curiosity led her to pause at the French doors for a moment.

The scene inside reminded her of a school lunchroom where students and faculty ate together. The only difference was that there were no girls among the teens.

Gabe had grown up around a bunch of headstrong older brothers who competed at everything. He would know how to handle these troubled boys.

Being an only child, Stefanie couldn't relate. She'd been the center of her parents' universe from the time she was conceived. To Gabe she must have seemed so spoiled, adamant on getting her own pampered way because she'd been given everything, and had never had to share.

Thanks to his father who planted the idea in Gabe's head a long time ago, Gabe honestly believed she had her heart set on being the First Lady one day.

How little he understood her!

All she'd ever wanted was to be *his* first lady, whether they were rich or poor, regardless of any and all circumstances. But with hindsight she could see that she had only herself to blame for giving Gabe the wrong impression.

She'd enjoyed working for his father, but it was only a job. If she could be Gabe's wife again, it was all she would ever ask of life. Somehow she had to find a way to show him she wasn't the person he thought she was.

If she could learn about the operation of the ranch, then she could help him and share his burdens, whatever they were. Getting a job in the barn was a step in the right direction, but that was only one part of the picture.

She also needed to become good friends with the staff and students inside the house. Gabe would notice right away if they were accepting of her. Then maybe he might see her in a new light. If only she could reach him so he would let down his defenses and admit he wanted and needed her in his life the way she wanted him…

It all had to happen in a couple of weeks!

While she got ready for town, she experienced the gamut of emotions until she felt feverish. By the time she hurried outside to Gabe's car, her adrenaline had kicked in, tripling her pulse rate.

Gabe still hadn't made an appearance with Clay. It was just as well. She needed time to calm down. When she tried the door to his Explorer and it didn't open, she took a little tour of the compound on foot.

There were three other log cabins set back in the pines to the left of the main ranch house. They looked new.

To think that every time Gabe had left Newport, he'd flown out here to supervise the building and remodeling of his ranch.

Don't forget his overnight stopovers in Providence.

As if thinking about Clay's mother had conjured him up, there was her son coming out of the middle cabin with Gabe's hand on his shoulder.

The teen was tall and lanky. All bones. He had dark brown hair and regular features, but he wouldn't grow into his looks for several years yet. If she'd seen the two of them together like this, she would have known they weren't father and son. It would have saved her a lot of unnecessary torture during her five-day trip across the country.

Unfortunately there was still the matter of the mother…

As the two of them approached, Gabe's veiled eyes met hers in silent greeting.

"Teri Jones? Meet Clay Talbot, our newest student."

"Hi, Clay. It's very nice to make your acquaintance."

The boy stared hard at her in what could only be described as teenage admiration. "Same here. Are you one of the staff?" His question sounded blatantly hopeful.

She refused to look at Gabe just then. "Not exactly. I've been hired to help out in the barn."

"Cool!"

"Ms. Jones needs some work clothes, too. Shall we go?" Gabe suggested in his deep male voice, but it sounded more like a command.

Clay started walking toward the car with her. "Anything would be better than the straitjacket I had to wear at military school," he muttered.

Stefanie flashed him a smile. "Don't knock it. I'll have you know women love a man in uniform."

"Yeah?" He cocked his head and smiled back. His smile was the charm. Just give him a little more time.

"You bet. If you have a picture of yourself in one, I'd like to see it."

His face flushed. "I might have a couple."

"Great. Pretty soon we'll get some more of you on horseback. Women like that rugged look, too," she confided. "You know, the cowboy hat and boots, the sheepskin jacket."

After Gabe opened the doors to his Explorer, she started to get in the back, but he gripped her arm and helped her into the front seat. Clay perforce had to climb in the back.

She could feel the negative tension radiating from Gabe. It set her heart knocking against her chest.

Why was he so upset? All she'd tried to do was make Clay feel more at ease. The teen was a long way from home and probably feeling it.

"Where's Clover? Can't we bring her with us?" Under the circumstances, the dog would be a great comfort to both her and Clay.

The forbidding man at the wheel shot her an enigmatic glance. "Not this trip. Ready, Clay?"

"Yes, sir."

CHAPTER FIVE

"WHAT do you think, Clay?"

Gabe had been reading a magazine published by the Western Cattleman's Association when Stefanie stepped out from behind the curtain at Herb's Saddlery and Outfitters in Kalispell.

"Wow!"

Wow was right.

Stunned by the vision that filled his eyes, Gabe forgot where he was or what he'd been reading.

That was his wife standing there in all her glory!

The gorgeous face beneath the cowboy hat crushing those alluring Gypsy curls at a jaunty angle was breathtaking enough. But did she have to look so damn beautiful in that tan Western shirt her slender curves did wonders for?

His gaze fell lower to the jeans only the flare of womanly hips and shapely long legs like hers could carry off. In cowboy boots she looked taller, more voluptuous somehow.

Judging by the small audience she'd attracted, the other shoppers and salespeople thought so, too.

In chiffon or leather, blond hair or black, with her classical bone structure there wasn't another woman on the planet who had such physical appeal and sophistication all rolled together in one enticing package.

"We ought to fit in with everyone else now," she

commented as she walked around Clay, studying his new brown Western outfit approvingly.

"Yeah." The smitten fifteen-year-old was blossoming before Gabe's very eyes. In Stefanie's presence, the pale, often sullen-faced teen had come to life.

"Yes indeed. You look mighty fine, Mr. Talbot. I say we ought to show you off. What do you think, Mr. Wainwright?"

Her eyes swerved to Gabe's. Amazing how her brown contact lenses hid all evidence of the heavenly blue color behind them.

"I noticed there's a time travel movie playing in town. Have you seen it?" she prodded.

The old Stefanie had never been deliberately provocative before. He didn't know this side of her existed. With her lethal brand of charm, it was no wonder her unsuspecting victims had been willing to part with hundreds of thousands of dollars to aid his father's cause.

He put down the magazine he'd stopped reading since she'd made her entrance, and stood up. "I don't think I've seen a movie in at least five years."

A tantalizing smile broke out on her lips. "Well then, boss—" she laid on the phony Western twang "—would you be willin to cut two new cowhands like us a little slack before we have to mosey on back to the ranch and knuckle down to business?"

Stefanie, Stefanie. Who are you?

"Is that what you'd like to do, Clay?"

His face lit up. "I'd love it! They didn't have videos or television at the academy, and we weren't allowed off campus."

The hint of pleading in Stefanie's eyes shouldn't

have come as any surprise to Gabe. He knew he'd been rough on her since he'd discovered she was the woman stuck in the ditch.

Part of his reaction had been pure shock that she wasn't in Europe, that she'd traced him all the way to Montana.

The other part had been pure anger at himself because his heart had acted up at the first sight of her.

To his chagrin, it showed no signs of quieting down. In fact he'd come close to suffering cardiac arrest when she'd walked out to model her new clothes in front of Clay.

That wasn't supposed to happen. None of this was supposed to have happened. He thought he'd closed the door on an unorthodox marriage that should never have taken place.

Now here he was once more, at the mercy of her dangerous power over him. *And loving it.* Which was a cardinal sin under the circumstances.

One movie. That was all.

When it was over, he would distance himself from her completely. In two weeks he'd put her on a plane home. That would be it!

"I've got a fence to repair before the day is out, but if we hurry, I think we could fit in a film."

Stefanie looked relieved. "Did you hear that, Clay? Grab your sacks and let's go."

When they reached the theater, Stefanie ran ahead and bought tickets for everyone before he could. You would have thought she was the teenager the way she loaded them down with treats and drinks.

Gabe purposely arranged it so Clay sat between them, but he soon regretted his mistake. Throughout the film, she and Clay whispered off and on as they shared popcorn.

Once in a while Gabe heard her husky laughter. It resonated to his insides. She and the boy were relating like mad. An easy camaraderie had sprung up between them. For a teen who'd had difficulty opening up to adults, Stefanie's impact on him was rather remarkable.

Apart from the situation with her and his father, Gabe had never been jealous of any one or thing. But he was feeling that treacherous emotion around his charge who'd claimed her complete attention.

During the drive back to the ranch, Stefanie commented that the swimming pool scenes where the boy dived into the water to pass back and forward in time were the best parts of the movie.

"Yeah, that was clever," Clay admitted, "but I thought it was cool that the boy had the hots for the high priestess of the island."

"Hardly the hots," Gabe countered, not liking the direction of the conversation.

"Mr. Wainright has a point, Clay. She was kind to him because he'd come from another world and had been separated from his mother. Naturally he felt affection for her. Don't forget she'd been dedicated to the gods and couldn't marry or have children, but she could protect him. It wasn't until he went forward in time and then came back to her world as a man that his feelings turned to love."

Her explanation had been so masterfully put, Clay had no comeback. But Gabe still felt shivers chase across his skin because the story could parallel the teen's situation at the moment. A little attention from a female, especially one who looked and acted like

Stefanie, could overwhelm a vulnerable boy on the brink of manhood.

As long as Gabe planned to distance himself from Stefanie, it would be wise to keep Clay away from her, too. A visit from the boy's mother was the thing her son needed most. *As soon as possible*. It would help him get over his feelings of abandonment.

Once they reached the main house, he noticed how Clay rushed to help Stefanie with her sacks as she got out of the car.

"Thank you, Clay."

"You're welcome. What are you going to do now?"

The expectant sound in his voice warned Gabe to intervene before Stefanie decided to take any more pity on him.

"Ms. Jones has her work cut out for her. So do we, Clay."

The boy's head jerked around. "What do you mean?"

"You're going to ride to the lower pasture with me. I'll teach you how to mend a torn fence."

The slight frown told a lot. "Why do you have to do that?"

"So the cattle won't stray to places where we can't find them and they starve to death. I'd be out of business if that happened."

"Whoa."

Gabe smiled. "Whoa is right." He turned his attention to Stefanie. "Thank you for treating us to the movie, Ms. Jones."

"Yeah. Thanks a lot," Clay piped up.

"It was my pleasure," she murmured, her gaze sliding from Gabe's to the boy. "You're a lucky guy to have someone like Mr. Wainwright show you the ropes. There's no man anywhere with more expertise. You'll learn things with him nobody else could teach you.

"Mr. Wainwright would deny it, but to many people he's a legend. I'll tell you something else—if I had to depend on one person out of the whole world for my survival, I'd choose him." She patted Clay's arm. "I just thought you ought to know how privileged you are to be in his company. See you around, Clay."

While she headed for the house, Gabe stood there in a trancelike state, not only shaken by her words, but by the conviction with which she'd said them.

Clay turned his head and looked at Gabe with fresh interest. There was a new degree of respect in his voice when he said, "I'll put my things in the room and be right back, sir."

"I'll be waiting."

Gabe's eyes closed tightly.

He'd lived with Stefanie for a year. He thought he'd known all there was to know about her. Today's outing proved he'd been way off base where she was concerned.

Like a chameleon, she seemed to adapt to any situation that came along. He hadn't seen that side of her in Newport.

Because being a socialite wife was the only part she'd been called upon to play? an inner voice nagged.

So far her acting ability brought authenticity to any role she chose. Was one part more real than another? If that was the case, which part?

For a half second in the saddlery, she'd had him

convinced she was really enjoying this whole cowgirl business.

Yet during her speech to Clay just now, a speech that had touched Gabe profoundly, he thought he'd heard regret in her voice for what might have been.

He groaned in turmoil. *Come on, Clay. I need to get out on the range where I can clear my head.*

With everyone at dinner, Stefanie decided to take a long, hot bath. It was a relief to shed her disguise.

While she'd been in town with Gabe and Clay, who was a delight, someone had brought her a lamp. They'd also put a lock on her bedroom door. No doubt Gabe had issued the order knowing how much she needed her privacy. Now she'd be able to sleep without her wig until she left the ranch.

The outing to Kalispell had been heavenly because she'd been able to spend the better part of a whole day with Gabe. She was glad Clay had gone with them. Otherwise Gabe would never have agreed to see a film.

And she would never have dared parade in front of him in her new clothes.

She'd taken a big risk in pushing Gabe as far as she had. But it had been worth it. Her body still throbbed from the look in his eyes when she'd first come out from behind the fitting room curtain. She'd seen desire before, but this time she'd watched that desire ignite into flame.

He wanted her. She'd felt his hunger in every atom of her body.

But how to get him to act on that want…

A half hour later she dashed down the hall to her room with a towel wrapped around her head. After locking the door, she turned on the light, then sat on the cot to blow-dry her hair.

As soon as she could brush it into a silky curtain, she found her cell phone and put in a call to Wes, one of the P.I.s. He didn't pick up, so she left a message on his voice mail to phone her parents and let them know she was all right.

Although she didn't dare tell them her location, it would have been cruel to allow any more time to go by without a word from her.

While she was taking the tags off her new shirts and jeans, she heard a rap on the door.

She lifted her head. "Marva?"

"It's Gabe."

Yes!

"I thought you'd be at dinner. We need to talk."

The coldness in his tone took away her excitement. Her heart began to thud outrageously. Maybe he was going to tell her he'd changed his mind and she would be leaving in the morning after all.

"J-just a minute."

Cinching the belt of her velour robe around her waist a little tighter, she gave the tiny room a cursory inspection. With all her things in it, there was hardly a place for him to stand.

Undoing the lock with a trembling hand, she opened the door. Because the hallway was shrouded in darkness, the only light came from the lamp in the corner. It revealed his chiseled features in stark relief.

His body seemed to still in place as his eyes wandered over her hair and features with relentless scrutiny. No longer in disguise, she could imagine how colorless she looked.

As if remembering that Marva or someone else

might see them, he made an unexpected move inside and shut the door, forcing Stefanie backward. She ended up sitting on the cot, her hands gripping the edge nervously.

His sudden intake of breath resounded within the intimate log walls. "Several things happened today you need to know about."

Averting her eyes she said, "If you mean I went too far in orchestrating things so Clay could see a movie, I'm sorry. I realize I know nothing about the legal ramifications of caring for these boys. I shouldn't have interf—"

"I'm glad you did," he cut in on her unexpectedly. "You reminded me of the old adage about all work and no play. For the past couple of years, Clay hasn't had much fun in his life. Your friendliness and acceptance brightened his world. If anything, I'm indebted to you.

"Depending on their behavior, I'm going to make certain the boys get to town once a week for the exact kinds of things we did today."

His words filled her with happiness. Unable to control herself, she found herself smiling up at him. "So, are you saying that even you had a good time?"

He slowly nodded. "Guilty as charged. You have a natural way with people. Men and boys in particular. My father believes you walk on water—"

She shuddered. *Not anymore he doesn't.*

"As for Clay—" Gabe continued, unaware of her chaotic emotions, "he's developed an oversize crush on you. The other boys have been given a detailed description and can't wait to meet the woman in the barn who's more beautiful than any movie star."

Heat washed over Stefanie in waves.

"That's what I wanted to talk to you about. Clay's vulnerable right now. Since you'll be leaving soon, I'd advise you to tread caref—"

"Don't worry," she interrupted, fighting not to break down in tears because he couldn't wait for her to be gone from the ranch. "I'll keep my distance with all the boys and treat everyone the same."

He raked a hand through his black hair, a gesture she'd seen him do on other occasions when he'd had something serious on his mind.

"That would be the best plan. There are eight students so far, four to each cabin with their own set of surrogate parents. Tomorrow I'll introduce you to the Clarks and the Millwards who live here year round and have been trained to serve in that capacity."

"Which of course *I* haven't," she muttered in a brittle tone. "For the record, I promise to stay in the background. Is there anything else?"

Lines darkened his handsome face, making him appear older. "I'm afraid so."

Her head flew back. "Obviously I've made another faux pas, or worse." She had to pause to catch her breath. "Is it Marva?"

His brows furrowed. "What do you mean?"

"I don't know. Last night she didn't seem very happy about me being here."

Gabe shifted his weight, making her unbearably aware of his potent sensuality.

"Marva hasn't discussed anything with me. If there's something wrong, I'm sure it has nothing to do with you. But rest assured I'll get to the bottom of it."

She bit her lip. "If this isn't about Marva, then you were probably going to warn me to leave Clover alone. I know very well how important it is for a watchdog to only have one master. But when she seeks me out, it's impossible to ignore her. She's been endowed with a loving nature, very much like my old golden lab, Mitzi."

"*You* had a dog?" He sounded incredulous.

"A succession of them from the time I was born. But Mitzi was my favorite."

"How come you never talked about her?"

"She got killed by a drunk driver on the day I graduated from high school. For a long time afterward I felt like I'd died, too. Mom and Dad ran right out to get a replacement for me, but I didn't want another dog unless it was Mitzi. I couldn't bear it."

Her eyes smarted in remembrance. "After that, I was away at college and the circumstances were never right to get another dog."

Gabe's chest rose and fell heavily. "While you're here, you're welcome to love Clover all you want."

"But—" she fired at him, knowing there was still something else he wasn't pleased about.

"You've met Mack."

She blinked. "And?"

"He's my right hand."

"Naturally, since he's your foreman."

"Before his wife died of cancer a year and a half ago, he was a rancher of a little spread in another part of the state. The medical bills soared. After the funeral he was forced to sell everything."

"That's horrible," she whispered.

"I agree. Since they were childless, he had nothing to keep him there, so he moved around working for various people, attempting to deal with his pain."

That's exactly how I felt when you left me, Gabe.

"When he saw the ad I ran in the newspaper, he applied for the job of foreman here. There were a lot of applicants, but for a variety of reasons he stood out head and shoulders above the rest.

"In truth I would have hired him for his ranching skills alone. But it was when he told me how much he'd wanted to have children, and was looking forward to teaching the boys those skills, I realized how fortunate I was to have him on board."

Stefanie had an idea where this conversation was headed and didn't like it one bit.

"What you're trying to say is that he's vulnerable, just like Clay."

"Yes," was Gabe's tight-lipped response. "You *are* an exceptionally beautiful woman, Stefanie. Your kind of looks are rare, and will always turn a man's head. I have no doubts Mack took one look at you and thought he was in love again."

"That's absurd!"

"Why else would he agree to take you on?" Gabe drove the point home. "As it is, the man requires all hours of the day he can find to accomplish everything needed doing around here. Tell me exactly what he said he was prepared to do for you."

She sucked in her breath. "I'm to report at seven every morning to get used to the horses and clean out the stalls."

"What else?" he demanded.

Uh-oh.

"H-he said he would give me riding lessons every day after lunch."

Gabe gave an emphatic shake of his head. "That's out."

"Well, since the stockmen and married men of

your staff are off limits, I guess that means *you* are the only member of the masculine gender around here who's impervious to my wiles.''

When that didn't get a reaction out of him, Stefanie grew more reckless. ''After a year of marriage when you never touched me, I guess I have unassailable proof.''

The tension crackled like a lightning storm between them.

''All the better then if *I'm* the one who teaches you the fundamentals of riding. That way we'll avoid any complications.''

''I'd say there's already a big one!'' she blurted in fresh pain.

''How so?''

''I've lived with you, remember? No one can get busier than you.''

''Don't worry. I'll fit you in.''

Her heart leaped. ''When?''

''When it's convenient.'' If he was intentionally trying to taunt her, he was doing a perfect job of it.

''In other words, never.''

From joy to despair in a matter of milliseconds. Stefanie couldn't take any more.

''On the contrary,'' his low voice sounded mocking. ''Spring is calving time. On Friday you can ride with me while I check on some of the cows near the river. If it's too strenuous for you, we'll find out in a hurry.''

She wouldn't put it past Gabe to take her on a monster ride into the mountains over boulders and snowdrifts, hoping it would put her off horses permanently. Then he wouldn't have to bother with her again.

But she loved him so much, she'd go with him and endure it, even if it killed her!

Wait— Friday was days away. In all probability, he would make himself scarce until then. Which gave her an idea...

She stirred restlessly on the cot. "What shall I tell Mack? About the riding lessons, I mean."

After a brief pause, "I'll thank him for accommodating you in the mornings, but let him know his offer to give you afternoon pointers goes way beyond the call of duty. On a personal level, he'll be disappointed as hell. Professionally, however, it'll be all right with him."

"That's good. So—do I assume my afternoons and evenings are free?"

"Of course. You can come and go as you please. No need to check in with Marva. Meals are served cafeteria style. It doesn't matter if you show up or not."

He couldn't have made it more explicit that the less anyone saw of her around the ranch house, including him, *especially him,* the better.

She had news for Gabe. He was going to get his wish!

"If you've come to the end of your long list, I find that I'm tired and would like to go to bed."

"It's the altitude," he said with unflappable calm. "By the time you've become fully acclimatized, your two weeks will be up. Good night, Ms. Jones. Sleep well." The door clicked shut.

Sleep well.

She threw one of her pillows at it with all her might.

Gabe heard a thump coming from Stefanie's room.

He paused midstride, wondering if her cot had collapsed. When there was no other sound, he continued down the hall to the dining room where Marva was finishing up last-minute details before going to bed.

"How are you doing, Marva?"

"I'm fine, Gabe." She kept filling the salt shakers. "You want another slice of peach pie?"

Stefanie was right. His cook did seem a little offish.

"Why do I get the feeling there's a burr under your saddle?"

She shook her head. "Pay me no mind. I just work here."

"So do I. By now I thought we were good enough friends that if something was wrong, you could come to me."

"I always have."

"Except for this time."

"This time it's none of my business."

"Then I give my permission for you to make it your business."

She put the big salt carton away and wiped off the counter. Halfway through, she squinted at him.

"I've been your greatest admirer from day one, so for the life of me I can't figure out why you put Teri Jones in that freezing old closet when there's a perfectly good guest bedroom upstairs!"

Stefanie had a champion and didn't know it.

"I like to keep that room open for one of the boys' parents, in case they drop in without calling first," he countered on a burst of inspiration. "Strictly speaking, Ms. Jones isn't a guest. She came to the ranch looking for work. I could hardly put her on the

An Important Message
from the Editors

Dear Reader,

Because you've chosen to read one of our fine romance novels, we'd like to say "thank you!" And, as a special way to thank you, we've selected two more of the books you love so well, plus an exciting Mystery Gift, to send you absolutely FREE!

Please enjoy them with our compliments...

Pam Powers

P.S. And because we value our customers, we've attached something extra inside...

Peel off seal and place inside...

EDITOR'S
FREE GIFT
SEAL
THANK YOU

How to validate your Editor's
FREE GIFT
"Thank You"

1. Peel off gift seal from front cover. Place it in space provided at right. This automatically entitles you to receive 2 FREE BOOKS and a fabulous mystery gift.

2. Send back this card and you'll get 2 brand-new Harlequin Romance® novels. These books have a cover price of $3.99 each in the U.S. and $4.50 each in Canada, but they are yours to keep absolutely free.

3. There's no catch. You're under no obligation to buy anything. We charge nothing—ZERO—for your first shipment. And you don't have to make any minimum number of purchases—not even one!

4. The fact is, thousands of readers enjoy receiving their books by mail from the Harlequin Reader Service®. They enjoy the convenience of home delivery...they like getting the best new novels at discount prices BEFORE they're available in stores...and they love their *Heart to Heart* subscriber newsletter featuring author news, horoscopes, recipes, book reviews and much more!

5. We hope that after receiving your free books you'll want to remain a subscriber. But the choice is yours—to continue or cancel, any time at all! So why not take us up on our invitation, with no risk of any kind. You'll be glad you did!

6. Don't forget to detach your FREE BOOKMARK. And remember...just for validating your Editor's Free Gift Offer, we'll send you THREE gifts, *ABSOLUTELY FREE!*

GET A FREE MYSTERY GIFT

YOURS FREE!

SURPRISE MYSTERY GIFT COULD BE YOURS _FREE_ AS A SPECIAL "THANK YOU" FROM THE EDITORS OF HARLEQUIN

Visit us online at
www.eHarlequin.com

couch in the living room where the staff likes to congregate at night. Right now she's on probation.''

Marva frowned. "Probation—"

"If she can't do the job at the barn, Mack will have to let her go."

"That barn's freezing in the morning!"

"Rain or shine, the work has to go on. You know that."

"Well if you ask me, which you haven't, it seems like she's being set up to fail."

He reached for an apple in the bowl and bit into it. Marva was more shrewd than he'd realized.

"If she does, it'll save me having to find a better place for her to sleep. She can't bunk with the stockmen. Let's be honest. I need people around here who can pull their own weight. That's one of the reasons I hired you."

His remark produced the friendly smile he was looking for.

"What's the other?" she quipped.

"Your sourdough bread. It's to die for. But you already know that."

"It's still nice to hear."

"As a matter of fact I love everything you make. So do the boys. There's no substitute for real home cooking. Your delicious food oils the wheels around here and keeps the inmates happy. Don't ever quit on me."

"I don't plan on it anytime soon."

Gabe stopped munching. "Are you trying to tell me something else?"

"No, of course not. But you never know when unforeseen circumstances will happen. Looking down the road, it probably wouldn't hurt to train another person.''

He blinked. "You have someone in mind?"

"Well—if Ms. Jones needs a job and it doesn't work out in the barn, maybe she'd like to try the kitchen."

Damn. He should have seen that coming. Stefanie's arrival had caused him to lose his edge.

She could make coffee and heat up frozen TV dinners, but he had no idea if she could cook or not. He'd gone to great lengths to keep their lives separate. As a result, they'd never eaten meals together at home. One thing was certain. The kitchen was the last place Stefanie planned to end up. The day would come when she would be conferring over menus with the White House chefs.

"I'll think about your suggestion for a helper. But let's put the idea of Ms. Jones on hold. It's possible she'll call it quits before the week is out and head for greener pastures."

Marva flashed him an enigmatic glance. "If you say so."

CHAPTER SIX

WHAT a difference in the weather from two days ago! Since the storm had blown itself out, Stefanie had seen nothing but sunshine. It was a relief to travel over dry ground and know she wouldn't get caught in another storm.

If memory served, the riding stable she was looking for had a name that started with a *D*. She recalled seeing it on the north end of Kalispell every time she'd been to the town.

One more bend in the road.

Dankers. That was it!

Excited by her find, she left the highway and pulled into the parking lot. But her spirits deflated when she walked over to the barn door and discovered the place was locked.

Her gaze shifted to the adjacent house. There was a pickup truck in the driveway. Maybe someone was home.

Not to be defeated, Stefanie climbed the porch stairs and pressed the buzzer. In a few minutes an attractive brunette woman probably in her late twenties answered the door. She gave Stefanie a friendly hello.

"Are you Mrs. Dankers?"

"Yes. Can I help you?"

"I hope so. My name is Teri Jones. Forgive me for disturbing you, but I've driven some distance to go riding. Actually I was hoping I could pay someone to teach me how to ride, or at least give me a few pointers. What are your hours? I didn't see a sign of any kind.''

"That's because we don't officially open until June.''

"Oh. I didn't realize.'' Stefanie had had such hopes! "Maybe you could tell me if there's another stable in the area where I could take some riding lessons?''

"There are several, but like us, they don't open much before summer when the tourists come.''

Ridiculous as it was, she found herself fighting tears. "I'm afraid summer will be too late for me, but thank you anyway. I'm sorry to have bothered you. Goodbye.''

Stefanie turned sharply away and started down the stairs.

"Wait!''

With pounding heart, Stefanie looked back over her shoulder.

"I've got a couple of hours I can spare before I have to pick up my daughter Mandy at school.''

"You'd be willing to teach me?'' Stefanie cried out in excitement.

"Sure. Why not. Let me grab my jacket and keys and I'll walk you over to the barn.''

Stefanie only had to wait for her a few minutes. As soon as she reappeared, Stefanie said, "Mrs. Dankers—I promise I'll make it worth your while. Name your price.''

The other woman smiled as they walked side by side. "It'll be the same as I would charge anyone else. The name's Pam.''

"Pam, you're wonderful! The thing is, I have a

confession to make. I need to learn how to ride by this Friday!''

"That far away, huh?'' the other woman teased.

Stefanie felt an immediate liking for her and laughed out loud. But when she remembered her mission, she sobered.

"It's very important. My boss has put me on two weeks probation. If I don't measure up, I'll be out of a job.'' She tried to swallow, but there was a boulder-sized lump in her throat. "I can't lose it. I just can't.''

Pam eyed her speculatively before unlocking the barn door. "If that's the case, you're going to need more than one lesson.''

"I know. My problem is, I work every morning and can't get away until noon. But after that, I'm free until bedtime.''

"I'm free at this time tomorrow. On Thursday I have to volunteer at school, but I'll get my husband, Hayden, to help you. One look at you and he won't mind a bit.''

The woman was pure gold. At this point Stefanie couldn't prevent the tears. "You'll never know what this means to me.'' Her voice shook.

"Mind if I ask a question before we get started?''

"Of course not.''

"How long have you been in love with your boss?''

Stefanie let out a quiet gasp.

"Hey—I was only kidding. I meant no offense.''

"I'm not offended,'' Stefanie assured her. "Your instincts must be infallible. I—I've loved him for a long time.''

Pam whistled. "This is serious stuff.''

"Yes," Stefanie chuckled in spite of her agony.

"Well then, you're going to get the crash course. You may not be able to take home the rodeo queen trophy by Friday, but we'll make darn sure you can hold your own!"

True to Pam's word, by the time Thursday night rolled around, Stefanie had been put through the paces and her body was paying for it. Between raking out the stalls in the morning, then putting hours in the saddle all afternoon, she couldn't tell which part of her anatomy hurt the worst.

To compound the problem, she always stayed in Kalispell after her lessons and ate dinner by herself. Then she would take in a movie before heading home. Anything to while away the time so she wouldn't have to face Gabe and explain where she'd been. As a result, her muscles tightened up on her before she had the chance to soak her aching limbs in a hot tub.

When her alarm went off Friday morning at six-thirty, she wanted to die she was so tired and sore. Here she'd been waiting, living for this day to come so she could spend it with Gabe, and now she could hardly move without moaning in physical pain.

She dressed with difficulty before staggering to the kitchen for a cup of coffee and one of Marva's fabulous cinnamon rolls. As she entered through the French doors, Gabe was just coming out. Anytime she saw him after deprivation, her heart turned over on itself.

His gaze made an intimate perusal of her face and body, scorching her with its intensity.

"Where have *you* been the past few days?"

He sounded angry. *Had he missed her?* Oh, how she hoped so!

"Driving around getting acquainted with the area." It wasn't exactly a lie.

"Until ten-thirty at night?" he derided.

So he *had* noticed. Her proud chin lifted. "I wasn't cavorting with anyone associated with the ranch, if that's what you're insinuating."

His expression looked like thunder. "I'm afraid you'll have to forego any extracurricular plans for today. That goes for the evening as well. In case you'd forgotten, you're riding with me to check the herd."

"I know."

"If there's a serious problem, we might have to make camp for the night. I'll come by the barn for you at eleven."

She looked down at the tip of her boots to hide the joy those words evoked.

"I'll be ready," she said in her meekest voice.

After a pregnant pause, he strode swiftly down the hall toward his office.

Stefanie found she was starving and ate a huge breakfast, much to Marva's satisfaction. When she'd finished a second cup of coffee, she returned to her room to grab everything she'd need for the outing. Then she headed for the barn on foot, aware of sore muscles with every step.

The boys had beaten her to it this morning. Mack had assigned each of them a job. Some were busy raking out the stalls. Others were learning how to adjust the automatic drip and fill the feed boxes with fresh alfalfa and timothy. Stefanie had been learning all the tasks along with them. She derived a lot of pleasure when Mack praised her for her work.

She chatted briefly with him and the boys before going to the tack room to hang up her cowboy hat and camera.

Clay followed her inside and shut the door. "Teri? Can I talk to you for a minute?"

For the moment they were alone. This was the kind of situation Gabe had warned her to avoid.

"Sure. Come on." She reached for a bridle. "You can help me with Molly. I'm going to be riding her today and need to check her hooves." Mack had taught Stefanie always to look for rocks or fungus before she ever mounted a horse.

Judging by the scowl on Clay's face, he didn't like the idea of them joining the others, but she'd purposely left him no choice.

He trailed her from the room to a stall halfway down the aisle. According to the foreman, Molly was the perfect little mare for Stefanie. Gentle, yet nimble with a lot of endurance.

"How's Molly this morning?" She gave the mare a hug around the neck. The horse nestled closer. "Say, I think you're ready for some exercise."

To Stefanie, the bridle was harder to put on than the saddle, but she finally managed it.

"There." She let out a deep sigh. "Now, Clay, if you'll steady her, I'll start to check her feet."

He grabbed the reins and hunkered down by her. In a hushed tone he said, "I've noticed you going out in your car a lot. I was wondering. Do you think you could find time this weekend to take me with you?"

She picked some gravel out of one hoof. "Mr.

Wainwright told me he has arranged to take you guys into town once a week.''

"I know, but we're not allowed to make any phone calls.''

"Then I couldn't let you do that, either, Clay.''

"Just one? I have to talk to Mom!''

Not for the first time did Stefanie agonize over the possibility that his mother was Gabe's lover. In case it was true, did Clay know?

"If it's that important, why don't you ask Mr. Wainwright to let you use the phone in the office? He's a very understanding man. I'm sure he'll say yes when you explain how urgent it is.''

"No.'' He shook his head. "You don't understand. He *can't* know about it.''

At this point Stefanie couldn't contain her curiosity. "Why not?''

"Because it would spoil everything.''

"What do you mean?''

"I want her to fly out here and surprise him.''

Stefanie closed her eyes tightly. "She'll probably make plans to visit you before too long, won't she?''

"Yes, but she needs to hurry!''

"Why?''

"I found out on the trip here that he and his wife just got a divorce.''

Aghast, Stefanie whispered, "He actually told you that?''

"Yeah. We talk about everything. He's the best. Mom says the same thing. If she knew about the divorce, then they could get married right away. I'd give anything for him to be my stepdad. Will you help me?''

She rose to her feet on unsteady legs. "I—I tell you what, Clay. I'll think about it and let you know."

"Thanks for not saying no," he muttered fervently.

"You'd better join the others now. We've both got work to do."

"Okay. Talk to you later."

After he walked off, she hugged the horse's neck once more, attempting to stifle her sobs. *What am I going to do?*

In a few minutes she'd pulled herself together enough to finish her chores. Pain caused her to work like an automaton, raising Mack's eyebrows more than once. At ten to eleven she carried an Indian blanket and saddle from the tack room to the stall.

The outing she'd been waiting for in breathless anticipation had been vitiated by a fifteen-year-old boy who was desperately attempting to put his broken world back together again.

Gabe had warned her that Clay was vulnerable. But she would wager not even Gabe knew to what degree Clay was counting on him for permanent security.

At this point the boy deserved to know Gabe's intentions where his mother was concerned. Otherwise the troubled teen might act out in ways that would put his future at greater risk.

Stefanie had one fear—to hear Gabe admit that he was in love with Clay's mother and planned on marrying her. But as horrifying as that reality would be, Stefanie had the moral obligation to broach the subject to Gabe who was legally responsible for the boy and felt great affection for him.

From what she'd gleaned listening to the boys talk,

they came from Montana and some of the surrounding states like Idaho and Wyoming. Clay hailed from Rhode Island, which made him the exception. It took no imagination to understand how flattered he would be by Gabe's attention.

There was a fine line between hero worship and love. No doubt many boys would straddle that line where Gabe was concerned. Clay had already crossed it.

What Clay didn't know was that Stefanie had ten years on him.

Gabe checked his watch. It was time to get Stefanie. Since he'd met her on her way into the dining room earlier that morning, the hours had passed with painful slowness. He intended to find out where she'd been spending her nights.

If he learned she'd been anywhere near the Branding Iron, then it meant some jerk cowpunk figured he'd died and gone to heaven when he saw her walk in the place.

Until Gabe drove her to the airport, there was no way in hell he would allow her off ranch property again. If necessary, he'd keep the gate locked around the clock.

With the saddlebag in place, Gabe mounted his gelding and rode out of the paddock toward the barn. Before he reached the entrance, he caught sight of Stefanie's gorgeous figure leading a saddled horse beyond the doors.

Mack knew that Gabe was taking Stefanie to inspect some heifers. He must have decided to help matters along.

Slowly Gabe closed in on her. She lifted her head.

Beneath the rim of her cowboy hat, a pair of lovely brown eyes he still wasn't used to focused on him, almost as if she were meeting him for the first time.

Neither of them spoke. A stillness had pervaded the atmosphere, catching him off guard. The next thing he knew she'd mounted the mare with her inimitable grace and was sidling over to him.

Anyone who didn't know her the way he did would assume she'd been born in the saddle. Either she'd learned to ride earlier in her life and had never told him, or someone had been giving her lessons.

He knew for a fact it wasn't Mack or any of the hands. That left one other possibility.

She'd been gone every afternoon and evening...

Pictures of some stranger with his hands all over her flashed through his mind. *All over the wife Gabe had never dared touch.*

Like wildfire, unbridled jealousy raged through him till he felt faint from the force of it.

"Are you ready?" He knew his voice sounded harsh but he couldn't help it. He needed physical exertion and lots of it before he would be able to calm down.

"Whenever you are."

The little tremor he sometimes heard devastated him. He was learning to read her—the brave voice that covered her vulnerability.

"Stay with me," he muttered.

"I'll try."

As he was to find out in the next hour, her *try* through forest and meadow exposed to the sun where the snow had melted into spots here and there, outdid most people's best efforts.

Stefanie's comportment in public had always been

impeccable. A source of great pride to him. But watching her handle Molly in that elegant, feminine way of hers took that feeling to a much deeper level.

So far Mack had been unstinting in his praise of her hard work in the barn. Secretly Gabe was touched by her determination to do her share, even to the point of finding a way to take riding lessons behind his back.

Though he kept a sharp lookout for strays, his gaze traveled repeatedly to her exquisite face. Gone was the picture of serenity he'd taken with him from Newport. In its place she exhibited an intensity that brought out new dimensions in her character. And new beauty.

She sat straight in the saddle, never complaining whether he changed the pace from a walk to a canter. Much as Gabe hated to admit it, the man who'd taught her how to ride had done a superb job. Even if she were hating this, Gabe had an idea she would keep going as long as he did.

"Let's head over to those rocks by the river. They're fairly flat and dry. We'll eat our lunch there."

"I—I didn't know you brought any." She sounded relieved.

"Riding can take more out of you than you think."

He'd given her an opening to admit she was tired and wanted to rest. Naturally she didn't say anything. But she didn't have to when he saw how hard she was trying to hide her stiffness as she dismounted by herself.

Gabe had learned to ride in his teens when his family let him and his brothers spend a month at a special dude ranch for VIPs in Colorado. Watching her now, he recognized all the signs of beginner's pain. After three straight days of lessons, she had to be in hell.

"I'll take care of the horses. You find us a spot to eat."

Out of the periphery he followed her progress while he tied the reins to a nearby pine tree where the horses could graze. Each step seemed to cause her agony.

Tamping down a smile, he removed the saddlebag and carried it to the slab where she sat with her legs dangling over the edge. Without her cowboy hat, the short black curls gleamed in the afternoon sun. As fetching as she looked, he wanted to see the golden silk beneath.

The blood pounded in his ears. He wanted to see all of her as nature had made her.

"The river's so swift!" she cried out at his approach.

"That's because of the spring runoff. In another month it will calm down enough for me to enjoy the best fly-fishing on earth."

Their gazes collided before she looked quickly away. He wondered if she was remembering anything about the evening when she found him on the shore in her father's boat.

Gabe had been out fishing, mulling over plans for the ranch in his mind.

Her appearance seemed to come from out of the blue, literally. His heart kicked over because he thought she'd sought him out for no other reason than she wanted to be with him. It would be a first.

When he saw the envelope and realized she was

on yet another errand for his father, he felt the same way he did when the boom of his sailboat unexpectedly knocked him into the ocean.

The feeling went much deeper than disappointment. From time to time Gabe had wondered if there might be something going on between her and his father.

Tormented by such unworthy thoughts, he'd always kept them to himself. But part of him lived in the secret fear that he might be jealous of his father's power over her.

He'd asked Stefanie to marry him because she was the only woman he had ever truly desired. And maybe part of him wanted his ring on her finger in order to keep her and his father apart. A test, if you will, to see if the closeness between the two of them was something more than affection.

Gabe received the answer to that question when she'd shocked him by agreeing to the marriage contract. At that point he realized the bond between his father and Stefanie could be summed up in one word—ambition.

She didn't want the father or the son. She wanted the office, the title, and everything that went with it. But she needed one or both of them to propel her on her way.

"Do you want me to help?"

Her voice with its hint of pleading jerked him back to the present. Since she'd come to Montana, he'd almost forgotten her true agenda behind this new *persona*.

Which brought him back to square one.

If her ambition had been that great, why had she followed him out here? In light of the seeming transformation in her, that question was starting to become a litany with him because he didn't have an answer.

"You must be hungry."

"I confess I am."

Her eyes widened as he began pulling their picnic from one of the pouches.

"Marva knows how to do it right. Bless her heart, she made the sandwiches with sourdough. There's fruit and chips. Help yourself." He reached into the other pouch for their sodas.

After devouring half a beef sandwich she cried, "This is ambrosia."

"Agreed." He drank a whole can of cola without stopping for breath. "So," he said when he put the empty can back into the pouch. "How long are you going to keep me in suspense?"

Color crept into her cheeks. "About what?" She quickly downed her drink.

"I'm impressed how well you've learned to ride, Stefanie. Who taught you? Where did you find him?"

"Her name is Pam Dankers."

Once again she'd shocked him by coming out with a different answer than the one he'd expected. He listened to her explanation with a niggling sense of shame for being totally off base. Again.

"Her husband Hayden filled in for her yesterday. He owns a feed store and had to get one of his employees to cover for him. I paid her the going rate, but I've got to think of a really nice way to show them my appreciation."

"If you'd like, you could invite them over to the ranch for dinner the night before you leave."

She turned her head toward the river. "That's very generous of you, but I don't think it would be a good idea."

"Why not?"

"I thought since your dad still doesn't know where you are, that you'd hoped to keep him in the dark a little longer. This couple could ask questions. They might even recognize you. If they were to spread the word, it could eventually get back to your father. That's all I'm saying."

"I appreciate your being so careful, Stefanie, but in this case I'm not worried about it." He handed her an apple, but she refused it. "Go ahead and ask them."

"Thank you."

"I thought you'd like to know Mack gives you highest marks for your work at the barn." As Gabe had feared, his foreman was already showing signs of infatuation.

"That's nice to hear."

"He says you're the hardest worker he's ever seen. I was glad to hear it because Marva told me she could use some help in the kitchen."

Stefanie's head shot around. "Is there something wrong with her?" The concern in her voice sounded genuine to Gabe.

"I'm not sure. She's probably picked up a bug. But now that you've learned the fundamentals of riding, I've decided you can split your time between the barn and the kitchen for the next week. If you were to offer to do the night setups for the next day, she could get to bed an hour earlier."

"Of course. I'll be happy to help out."

"Good." He started putting everything else back

into the pouches. "Just a word of caution—Mack's concerned about Clay's crush on you and feels you might be showing him a little too much attention around the other boys. Apparently this morning he went into the tack room with you and—"

"And what?" She rounded on him. Indignation had whipped fire into her cheeks. "He's got a crush all right, but it's not on me! I'm glad you mentioned him because there's something vital *you* need to know."

His brows knit in a frown. Clay was a complicated kid. "Go on."

"He likes you a lot, Gabe," she said in a quiet voice.

"That's because you haven't seen him angry yet."

"I'm being serious."

"So am I," his voice grated.

She faced him squarely. "This morning he sought me out for a favor."

"So Mack was right."

"Only partially. Clay wanted me to drive him to town so he could phone his mother without your knowledge."

He absently rubbed his thumb along his bottom lip. "I presume he gave you a reason."

"Yes." A haunted look crept into her eyes. "He wants her to fly out here right away."

Gabe had already been working on that. But it meant Madelaine needed to be sober by the time she arrived.

"Why didn't he tell me this himself?"

"You don't know?" Her cry of exasperation resounded in the meadow. Something was going on here he needed to get to the bottom of.

"Know *what?*"

She rubbed her forehead. "Clay said you told him that you had recently d-divorced your wife."

Oh, hell.

"That's true," he muttered at last. "I did."

Her breathing grew shallow. "According to him, y-you and his mother are on very close terms."

"It's par for the course since I've been her attorney for two years representing Clay."

"Apparently he thinks it's more than that."

"*How* much more?"

She got to her feet and looked down at him. "Do I have to spell it out for you? He wants you to be his new stepdad. The boy is desperate for her to get here and marry you before you find another woman to love. That's the crush I was referring to," she added in a quiet tone before climbing off the rocks.

Stunned by the revelation, Gabe was slow to move from his position. When he finally reached his horse, Stefanie had mounted hers and was waiting for him.

"I'll talk to Clay." With so many emotions tearing Gabe apart, those were all the words he could manage for the moment.

"How far is it till we find some cows?"

"Another half hour's ride."

He shoved his hat on his head. As if by tacit agreement, both horses moved forward at the same time.

Gabe had ridden over his land many times, always experiencing a sense of exhilaration and rightness. But the news about Clay had weighed him down, changing the tenor of their outing.

He wondered what thoughts were brewing in Stefanie's mind. They seemed to be as dark as his because she didn't speak again until they'd followed the curve in the river.

"I see cows! Oh—look at all the babies!"

In spite of his dark mood, he chuckled at her exuberance. "That's the idea. These are brood heifers. They'll be delivering calves all month."

His gaze took in the fifty-odd head of half-longhorns grazing pretty much together.

"I'm going to ride through the herd and see if any of them are in trouble. You wait here."

"I want to come, too."

His heart rate picked up as she sidled over to him. At his signal they moved forward together. If she was nervous, it didn't show. On the contrary, she acted excited. In turn, that excitement infected him.

He ran a trained eye over each animal, watching for signs of a heifer in distress. So far so good.

"Do they always have their babies out in the open like this?"

"For the most part. These are Texas longhorns. Ninety percent of the herd will deliver their calves without help. It's the other ten percent we have to worry about."

It wasn't until they made it through to the opposite side of the herd that he spotted a cow down near the fence.

"Gabe?" Stefanie called to him. "Look over there!"

"I've seen her. Come on."

He cantered as near as he dared, then dismounted. Stefanie followed suit. They tied their reins to the fence, then walked over to the heifer. Gabe knelt down next to her. Stefanie joined him.

"Oh...she's having her baby right now!"

"She sure is," Gabe muttered, noticing the feet sticking out but nothing else happening. "The knee of the mother's leg is bent. Do you see that? The calf can't get out."

Stefanie's eyes filled with tears as she looked at him. "We have to do something for them."

"We will."

Gabe got as close to the mother as he could and forced the bent leg to straighten.

"If you want to help, grab one of the calf's legs. I'll pull on the other."

Stefanie didn't hesitate. Together they began tugging. Slowly the head and shoulders appeared.

"Stop a moment. Let's see if mama can finish the job by herself."

They waited for a few minutes.

She shook her head. "I think she's too tired."

"I do, too," he concurred. "Keep pulling."

It didn't take much effort to deliver the rest. As soon as the calf lay in the grass, Gabe leaned over to see if it was breathing.

"What's wrong?" she cried in panic.

"Not a thing. I simply had to make sure she was breathing on her own."

The mother suddenly pushed him out of the way and began licking her baby.

"Oh, Gabe—" By now Stefanie was in tears which turned to sobs of pure, unadulterated joy. "We just helped that darling little calf get born— It's the most miraculous thing I've ever witnessed in my life!"

Gabe shared her emotions. Without conscious

thought he pulled her toward him, crushing her in his arms. They clung in an embrace he'd only been able to dream about until now.

In a minute she lifted a tear-ravaged face to his. "What if we hadn't come out here today? What would have happened?"

"Don't even think about it," he muttered before burying his face in the side of her neck. The fragrance of her skin intoxicated him.

For the next hour he held her close while they watched the calf sit up so he could be cleaned by his mother. Eventually he got up on all fours and began nursing.

Stefanie's tears dripped onto his cheek.

"The calf is so sweet! We have to give her a name."

"You mean *him*. Go right ahead." Gabe was too choked up to say anything else.

"I'm going to call him Lucky."

A chuckle escaped. "That sounds like a horse's name."

"I don't care. They both would have died without your help. You were wonderful. You knew exactly what to do. You always know the right thing to do." Her voice trembled.

He closed his eyes tightly.

Later, she turned to face him once more. "There must be other cows in trouble."

"I'm sure of it. That's why the stockmen are out checking all the herds around the clock."

She blinked. "Do you have a lot?"

"Quite a few."

"Are we going to keep looking, too?" She sounded so hopeful, he didn't have the heart to disappoint her. In truth, he was loath to return to civilization.

"It's getting late. After a wash at the river, we'll head for an old fire watchtower the forest service doesn't use anymore. En route you can help me keep an eye out for more strays. When dinner's over, we'll bed down there for the night and continue our search tomorrow on the way back to the ranch."

Later he saw her pull out her pocket camera. Again his heart was touched as she took half a dozen pictures of what she affectionately called mother and son.

CHAPTER SEVEN

"THIS place has all the comforts of home!"

Since they'd eaten chili and hot cocoa over the Coleman stove, Stefanie had enjoyed the freedom of walking around without her wig or contacts.

She continued to examine the interior of the roofed tower in delight. Gabe had caught back the shutters to make it open-air. The glow from the butane lantern revealed a walk-around porch. Before dark she'd been able to look over the railing to the ground thirty feet below.

Gabe had pumped up one air mattress and was working on the other. "After I bought the ranch, I had this structure repaired, then stocked it with bedding and supplies. If the hands ever get caught in a storm coming down this side of the range, they know they can find shelter here.

"As for the boys, this is their reward for good behavior. Some get to come here every couple of weeks for an overnight."

The stars from this vantage point looked like diamonds heaped on black velvet. "I was just thinking what an exciting hideaway this would have been when I was a girl."

"More exciting than your father's yacht?"

She heard an edge to his question, the first evidence of tension since they'd left the calf suckling. The beauty of that hour, the physical closeness they'd shared was something she would treasure forever.

"There's no comparison between the two. It's another mansion on water, not in the least imaginative. Up here you can pretend to be a thousand different things."

"Like what?" he mocked dryly.

"Rapunzel."

"What shall we be tonight I wonder?" His whimsical question threw her.

Emboldened by the intimacy of the night she said, "Peter Pan and the boys?"

His soft laughter resonated through her body. When it stilled he said, "Do you want children one day? During our marriage I don't believe the subject ever came up."

Gabe had no idea how cruel his question was. She sat down on the camp cot to pull off her cowboy boots.

"If the right man came along, I'd love seven or eight," she answered honestly.

"That many."

"Maybe it's a slight exaggeration, but I was an only child, don't forget. Mom always had to ship in friends for me. You can't imagine how much I envied you and your brothers. You never needed friends because you always had each other. When you got sick, you were all sick together."

"Don't remind me." He handed her an air mattress, which she put on her cot. "But I have to tell you that a First Lady with seven or eight children would be the sensation of the millenium."

Not that again! It appeared Gabe was a chip off the old block, only more impossible and stubborn than his father! Out of anger, she played along. "You're right, especially when I would insist we live elsewhere."

"I thought you told me it was every woman's dream."

"Of course it is. For entertaining dignitaries. But it's hardly the place to raise seven or eight children. One pillow fight and the Lincoln bedroom would be destroyed. Besides, children like things cozy.

"Did I ever tell you how much I hated my parents' house? It was too enormous for three people. Having a whole suite to myself scared me to death. For years I took my quilt and laid down by my parents' bedroom door at night, when they were home. They never knew I was there."

"Stefanie—" His whisper held shock and incredulity.

"There you have it." She laughed in remembered pain. "A page from the diary of a rich little Newport society girl who's all grown up now."

"But probably still terrified to sleep alone in her own suite," he muttered in self-deprecation. "Why didn't you tell me?" he ground out.

"And have you think I was trying to inveigle myself into your bed?" her question rang out in the brisk night air. "Gabe—I got over those fears when I went to college."

He handed her a couple of blankets. "I don't think so. Otherwise you wouldn't have come running to me when you should have been taking a well deserved vacation around the world."

"That's different." She lay down on the mattress and pulled the blankets up to her chin, ready to go to bed. "The world should be seen with a lover."

He moved around doing a few last-minute projects, then turned off the lantern. "I tend to agree with you." He got into his makeshift bed. Their cots were next to each other, the closest they'd ever been for a whole night.

While she was contemplating his comment, imagining herself locked in his arms in a Parisian attic, a mournful cry sounded out of the quiet.

"What was that?" Stefanie shot straight up in the cot.

"A coyote. It won't bother us."

"I'm sure it won't... Gabe?"

"Yes?"

"Thank you for bringing me today. I know you didn't want to, but I wouldn't have missed it. B-before you fall asleep, could I ask you one question?"

"Fire away."

She'd annoyed him again, but she wouldn't be able to settle down until she had an answer.

"Are you going to tell Clay I revealed his confidence to you? It's all right if you do, of course," she hastened to assure him. "You have to do what you think's best. I'd simply like to know what to expect the next time I see him."

"I plan to be straight with him."

Her breath caught. "So what you're saying is, he might turn on me."

"It's possible. But his wrath doesn't usually last very long."

"Since I'll be leaving in a week, I guess it's rather a moot point."

"Stefanie?"

"Yes?"

"If he makes you uncomfortable, come to me at once. I want that understood."

"I will." She couldn't take much more.

"Have you decided where you're going to look for work?"

She could scarcely breathe for her anguish.

"Probably Kalispell. Hayden said he could put me on part-time at the feed store if my job at the barn didn't pan out. But as I told you before, should I stay in the area, I promise I won't come to the ranch.

"When you and Clay's mother get married, neither she nor her son need know I'm anywhere in the vicinity."

"Did I say I was going to marry her?" came the terse demand.

What had Stefanie said to anger him now? "No, bu—"

"But nothing! Clay's desires have little to do with reality. I'm hoping that in time, the therapy he's getting here will help him to face certain truths and deal with them in appropriate ways."

"You're talking about his father's death."

"I mean the fact that his mother is an alcoholic, although she won't admit it."

No wonder Gabe wasn't rushing into marriage with her yet! Stefanie's throat constricted. "How tragic for both of them."

"That's the whole point, isn't it? Clay would probably get back on track much sooner if Madelaine were also in counseling."

"He has so much faith in you, I can see why he would think marriage to his mother would solve their problems."

"Many people waste their time wishing for things

when they ought to be working on the part of their lives they can do something about.''

A sharp pain attacked her heart, reverberating through her body. It sounded like Gabe understood all about Stefanie's hopeless love for him, and was telling her a few home truths for her ultimate good.

''Clay's very blessed to have someone like you in his life.'' She took a fortifying breath before venturing another question. Though she risked a rebuff or worse, her curiosity had become insatiable. After tonight there might never be another opportunity to talk this openly with him again.

''Gabe? Why did you set up the ranch?''

He must have changed positions on the cot because she heard the rustle of blankets. ''The first time our family traveled to Africa on one of Father's goodwill missions. He took us all over the world on various volunteer projects.''

''It's an amazing legacy he gave your family.''

''You're right. He taught us service. The only problem was, we could only give it for two or three weeks at a time. We'd just get started on a project, like helping a community get back on its feet after a flood, then it was time to fly home.

''Sometimes I felt like we shouldn't have gotten started in the first place. Our presence represented hope. In reality we only gave token assistance because we would have to pull out again before any long-term good could be done. We never saw anything through.

''I don't know the exact moment it came to me, but by my twenties I'd made up my mind to find one project and give it all I had. The next step was to earn a lot of money so I could fund it the way I wanted.''

Riveted by his explanations she asked, "How did you decide to help troubled teens?''

"By accident. I have a second cousin who would have gone to jail for possession of narcotics if the family hadn't come to me for legal help. The more he confided in me, the more I realized the pain he'd been in.

"It dawned on me then that it's easier to help airlift food and distribute it to pockets of hungry people, than it is to help someone in an emotional morass who might require years of counseling before they're on their feet again. That's where the idea was born.''

She raised up on one elbow. "When the day comes that your father learns about this place, I'll tell him he's to blame. He exposed you to the suffering in the world. You simply followed his example and took it to another level.''

"He'll write me off and you know it.''

"Surely he'll come around with time,'' she tried to encourage him.

"He might.''

In the next breath he reached out and caressed the side of her cheek with his hand. He'd never made a physical gesture like that toward her before. Her sense of wonder turned to longing. She would have kissed his hand if he hadn't withdrawn it and rolled away from her.

Finally she understood the reason why Gabe had walked away from a heritage that could have turned him into the most powerful man in the world.

But power was the antithesis of what Gabe was about. He had one driving need only—the desire to help those less fortunate than himself on a one-to-one basis. It translated to animals as well as humans.

All this time she'd been looking beyond the mark when the answer had been right there in front of her, so simple!

While those around him clamored to plan out his life, he'd been busy using his talents and means to obey a higher call. One to which he'd committed with such unwavering single-mindedness, he'd even married Stefanie in order to achieve his goal.

Gabe was so right to handle things the way he'd done up to now. The father he loved would never understand or approve. Because she knew the senator so well, she could hear his argument.

"Good Lord, son—you want to help people? What do you think being President of the United States means? How about effecting a peace treaty between warring nations, which would bring relief to millions of people throughout the world?

"How can you compare that kind of a good to dealing with a mere handful of spoiled rotten teenagers who will probably end up in prison no matter how many intervention techniques you apply?"

If that were all the senator was upset about, Stefanie could sympathize with his argument. But Gabe's father was an ambitious man who loved the power, the control, the excitement that went along with the position. He was a proud man who wanted those same things for his brilliant son.

It was never going to happen…

"Good night, Gabe."

The honk of Canada geese acted like an alarm clock for Gabe. While Stefanie was still out for the count, he stole from the cot and spent the next half hour making preparations for their departure. He left a breakfast of fruit and granola bars within her reach.

Once the shutters were closed, he descended the ladder to saddle the horses. Morning mist lay thick on the ground. Before Stefanie joined him, now would be the time to make a certain phone call.

It was almost 10:00 a.m. in Providence. If by some miracle Madelaine wasn't hung over, he would impress upon her the need for action.

He pulled his cell phone from the saddlebag and pressed the digits. To his chagrin her answering machine was on. *Damn.*

After the beep he said, "Madelaine? It's Gabe. Your son is not in physical danger, but something extremely serious has come up. It's vital that you fly out to Montana as soon as possible, preferably in the next twelve hours. I'm giving you my cell phone number again. Call me ASAP. I'll arrange for your flight and pick you up at the Glacier airport."

By the time he'd made check-in calls to Mack and the Wrigleys, his husband and wife psychologist team in charge of the boys on a twenty-four-hour basis, he could hear Stefanie calling to him. Satisfied all was well at the moment, he stuffed the phone back into the bag and climbed the ladder.

When he saw her blond head peering down from the porch railing, he was reminded of their conversation before they'd fallen asleep.

A true-life Rapunzel had indeed slept here last night.

But much as he didn't want to see her hide all that profusion of gold silk beneath the black wig again, attractive as it was, he knew it was for his own good.

At war with himself, it had taken every ounce of self-control he possessed not to drag her to the floor and make love to her till the birds warbled their morning song.

He sucked in his breath. Another night like last night and to hell with the rules he'd sworn not to break!

Judging by her extraordinary adaptability, he'd almost been persuaded that she liked ranch life.

Like a fool, there were moments yesterday when he'd come to believe she desired him for himself, nothing else.

But then she'd started talking about his father, how she would manage him when he learned Gabe's secret. He'd heard warmth and affection in her voice. As if it were a given that she was ready to take up her old life and pursue her dream the moment the six months were up.

Grim-faced, he reached the porch just as she was taking pictures. "Say cheese," she aimed her camera at him. "Without evidence, I might think our sleep-over was a figment of my imagination."

He stepped past her, not wanting to be reminded of a night he preferred to forget. She followed him inside.

"You haven't eaten yet," he muttered.

A crestfallen expression broke out on her face. "I didn't realize we were in a hurry. I'll be ready to go in five minutes!"

On went the cowboy boots and the wig. While she put in her contacts, he folded up her bedding to store. Out of the corner of his eye he saw her devour a bar before she stashed the rest of the food in her sheepskin jacket.

When she'd disappeared, he gave her a few minutes alone before he shut the door and started down the ladder.

In her cowboy hat seated astride Molly, she looked as if she belonged out here. The breathtaking picture she made beneath the pines tore his gut apart. He turned abruptly away and mounted Caesar.

"Follow me. We're going to proceed single file along an old Indian trail. It's a shortcut to another meadow, taking us only ten minutes instead of an hour. As soon as I've inspected that herd, we'll head back to the ranch."

She was unusually quiet as they made their way up an incline through tall timber. Wondering if she was afraid, he looked back and discovered her munching on an apple, appearing to be very much at one with nature.

Gabe didn't check on her again until the trail ended in a clearing and he heard an awe-filled gasp directly behind him. The enraptured look on her face, in her eyes, was the real thing.

He'd had the same reaction the first time he'd viewed this part of the ranch from the plane. A broad green meadow of contented cows surrounded by dark pines, with snow-capped mountains rising to an impossibly blue sky.

Stefanie's gaze finally left the vista to stare straight at him. "All it would take for your father to understand would be for him to hear Clay's praise of you, and then view *this*—"

The throb in her voice revealed enough emotion to move him to the deepest recesses of his soul.

"Whether he does or not is of no consequence."

Her eyes searched his. "That's a harsh thing to say."

Forever loyal to the senator. That was because Stefanie and his father shared the same dreams.

"He's a harsh man."

"He's afraid."

Her observation was as unexpected as it was shocking.

"We *are* talking about my father..."

"Yes." She stood her ground. "He adores you, but he's frightened of what he doesn't understand. He doesn't understand *you*. It's been his ultimate frustration, so he's come off like a tyrant."

Gabe's eyes narrowed on her features. "He confided this to you?"

She shook her head. "No. He didn't have to."

He didn't agree with her assessment, but there was no doubting her conviction. In recent years she'd spent more time around his father than almost anyone except his own siblings.

Perhaps she would answer the question that had kept him awake nights. "You were born into a family that has rubbed shoulders with prominent politicians for several generations. When there were so many possibilities to choose from, what prompted you to go to work for *my* father?"

A seductive smile curved her mouth, bewitching him. "You would have to be a woman to understand."

"Try me anyway!" he bit out, irritated because of his fatal attraction to her.

"No one else had four handsome sons. Didn't you know the Wainwright boys were legendary?"

"Don't trifle with me, Stefanie."

Her smiled faded. "I wouldn't do that."

He lurched forward in the saddle, exasperated by her answers.

"Except for me, the other three were already married by the time you came on the scene."

"That's right."

When her words sank in, an angry laugh rose in his throat. "You expect me to believe *I'm* the reason you went to work for Dad?"

She didn't move a muscle. "You'd be surprised at the strength of a girlhood crush." On that note she cantered toward the herd without him.

Gabe sat there in a quandary wondering how much of what she'd just told him was serious and how much was teasing. Was it possible he'd misjudged her relationship with his father?

Once more his gaze took in the pastoral scene, but suddenly he couldn't see Stefanie. He got a pit in his stomach when he spotted Molly near the edge without a rider.

Afraid Stefanie had been thrown, he urged Caesar to a gallop. When he got close enough, he dismounted, leading his horse by the reins. By the time he reached her kneeling figure, he could see a lifeless new calf in the grass.

"It won't move!"

Gabe was so thankful Stefanie was all right, the thrust of her cry barely registered until he hunkered beside her to examine it.

"This poor little guy didn't make it."

"Why?" This time her face was awash with tears of a different kind.

"Any number of reasons. Maybe his lungs didn't

clear of fluid. After the vet has a look, we'll get answers.''

"The mother's still licking her. She thinks it's going to get up." Stefanie sounded devastated.

"Come on. Let's go home." He gripped her arm. "I'll send a couple of stockmen to take care of him."

Once Stefanie had mounted, he climbed on Caesar and took another look around. He counted twelve new calves for the day. Eleven had survived and were nursing.

"Are you all right?" he asked later. They'd stopped to drink water and finish up the snacks in the saddlebag.

"That's the question I've wanted to ask you. It must be hard to lose any of them."

Stefanie understood a great deal.

"It's a cattleman's nightmare. But there are many more rewards. We'll be passing near an ancient watering hole shortly. Keep your eyes out and you'll see deer, maybe even some elk if we're lucky."

"My camera's ready."

Two days later Stefanie drove to Kalispell after lunch to get her film developed. She didn't look at the pictures until she'd arrived back at the ranch. Then she locked herself in her room where she was able to feast her eyes on the only man she would ever love.

She'd felt so close to Gabe during their overnight outing, she'd finally been daring enough to tell him the truth about her reasons for working for his father. But he'd thrown that love right back in her face because he patently believed she had other motives than wanting him for himself.

As for his involvement with Clay's mother, he

didn't give anything away about his personal feelings toward her. Just because she drank too much didn't preclude desire or love on his part.

Stefanie was desperate. She had less than a week before Gabe expected her to be gone from the ranch. Short of embarrassing them both by showing up in his bedroom uninvited and crying out her love for him, she didn't know how else to reach him.

While she lay on the cot dissolved in tears, her cell phone rang. Assuming it was one of the P.I.s, she clicked on and said hello.

"Teri? It's Pam."

"Pam!" Stefanie slid off the cot and got to her feet. "I was going to call you before the day was out."

"I'm glad I got to you first. I was just checking to find out if all our efforts paid off."

"My boss said he was very impressed. He gave full marks for the person who taught me. That's high praise coming from him. Thanks again for all your help."

"If you're able to keep your job, then that's all the thanks I want."

"Would you believe he's asked me to pitch in in the kitchen as well as the barn?"

"That's terrific, Teri. Tell me about the ride."

Stefanie gripped the phone tighter. "It was beautiful. I helped a calf get born. Then we c-camped out at a fire watchtower."

"Well, well, well. I had no idea it was going to be an overnighter. I'd say that's definite progress."

"I wish I could tell you it had been like that—" Stefanie's voice shook "—but nothing could have been further from the truth."

"What's the matter with the guy? Is he blind, deaf and dumb?"

Pam's reaction brought Stefanie close to tears again. "I—I think he might be in love with someone else."

"Then you've got to find out quick! I tell you what. Tonight there's a party at the church. It's our annual April 10 barbecue. Why don't you come with us and we'll help you devise a plan."

Stefanie blinked.

That meant tomorrow was April 11. *Gabe's birthday.*

"Pam—I wish I could come, but I have to work. Still, your phone call has already given me an idea. Thanks for being such a good friend. I promise I'll call you in a couple of days."

"I'll be waiting to hear from you. Good luck with you know who. Talk to you soon."

On fire with a plan that would involve everyone at the school in the celebration, she clicked off and hurried to the kitchen to consult Marva. The cook's excitement over giving Gabe a surprise party told Stefanie a lot about the woman's affection for him.

They spread the word to the staff. The following afternoon Stefanie slipped over to the school with some props in hand. Having obtained permission from the teachers ahead of time, she entered the cabin to talk to the boys.

Clay flashed her a private smile of greeting. It was full of hope that she'd decided to grant him the favor he'd asked for. Unfortunately it wasn't going to happen.

"You guys thought you were going to have an American history lesson today. Well, the plans have been changed. I'm here to teach you something else."

The boys burst into applause. There were grins all the way around.

"Do any of you know the definition of the word 'etiquette'?"

One hand went up. "It means something to do with manners."

"You're exactly right, Gary. Today you're going to learn the proper manners for eating at a restaurant. By the time I'm through with you, you'll be able to dine with a king in a royal palace and feel perfectly at ease.

"Of course that experience probably won't ever happen to you, but at least you'll impress the girls when you take them out on dates to a nice restaurant."

That comment captured their attention in a hurry.

"You need to be fast learners because tonight we're having a surprise birthday party for someone special. But you won't find out who it is until we assemble for dinner.

"You'll need to dress in shirt and ties for the occasion. I want you to make an impression. Okay, let's get started. Gary? Since you knew the answer, I'm going to make you my guinea pig. Come up to the table by me."

The boys hooted as the thin blond teenager got out of his seat and started toward her.

"Laugh if you want, but you're all going to have to take a turn at this. The first thing you must learn is how to seat a lady properly. You'll each be assigned a woman from the staff whom you'll assist at dinner tonight.

"After a run-through, I'll show you what to do with your napkin and then explain the use of each piece of cutlery. It's easy to learn and makes you feel confident in public. That's the whole point of this exercise. Tonight we really want to enjoy ourselves."

The boys seemed eager to comply. The hour passed quickly. Everyone had fun. Even the husband and wife team who taught the class got in the act.

When her presentation was over, she started gathering her supplies. Clay hung around to help her.

"It's for Mr. Wainwright, isn't it?" he whispered.

She imagined all the boys suspected as much. "You'll have to wait until tonight to find out."

"This'll be perfect! Yesterday he told me he got a call from my mom. She flew out today. He went to pick her up at the airport. She'll be here in time for the party. It looks like I don't need that favor from you after all."

Stefanie felt like the floor had just given way.

The advent of Madelaine Talbot's arrival at the ranch on this special night spelled the end of her dreams.

"I'm glad for you, Clay."

CHAPTER EIGHT

GABE escorted Madelaine into the living room of the ranch house. Clover raced over to greet him. He rubbed her head while he silently thanked God once more that Clay's mother had gotten off the plane sober.

His lecture over the phone had produced the wanted result. He needed her looking and acting like the responsible parent he knew she could be.

If he could get her to stay long enough for some counseling and family therapy with her son, maybe she would agree to attend Alcoholics Anonymous when she flew back to Providence. It would be a start in the right direction.

"Sit down by the fire. I'll find Clay so you two can have a reunion in private."

"Thank you, Gabe." She squeezed his hand in gratitude, then let him go.

"Come on, girl."

He left the living room and walked down the hall to the French doors, hungry for the sight of Stefanie. She was like a fever in the blood, growing hotter and hotter.

"Surprise!" everyone shouted as he entered the dining room to a standing ovation.

He came to a complete standstill. Marva beamed at him. "Happy Birthday from all of us, Mr. Wainwright."

Birthday...

He'd actually forgotten.

It was the same dining room with the same people. But everything had been transformed. The tables were set with white cloths. Fresh flowers and candles formed the centerpieces. A huge birthday cake had been placed on an extra table in the center of the room.

Everyone had dressed up, especially the boys who were behaving like real gentlemen.

This had to be Stefanie's doing. No one else knew. His heart began giving him a real workout.

His eyes searched the room for her. Clover found her before he did. She was standing behind the counter in the kitchen getting the food ready. He could tell she was purposely refusing to look at him.

"To say I'm pleasantly surprised would be a gross understatement. Thank you all for going to so much trouble for me. It means more than you know. But since I can tell you boys are starving, I'll cut the speech and ask that the festivities begin!"

After the students cheered and started taking their places, he signaled to Clay. "Your mother's in the living room waiting for you. If you don't feel like joining us, that's fine. Do whatever is comfortable for both of you."

"Thanks. You're the greatest."

As Gabe followed the teen's departure from the dining room, he knew Clay wouldn't feel that sentiment much longer. On the trip back from the airport, Gabe told Madelaine about Clay's conversation with Stefanie.

Now the ball was in Madelaine's court. She'd promised to tell Clay that she and Gabe could never be anything more than good friends. Mother and son had a lot of talking to do. Gabe hoped for a positive outcome, but he wasn't holding his breath.

Since he'd put Stefanie to work in the kitchen, it didn't raise anyone's eyebrows that she was assisting Marva. But instead of the dinner being served cafeteria style, their jubilant crowd was going to be waited on tonight. There were menus at each place offering a surprising list of items to choose from.

Again he saw Stefanie's hand in everything.

She chatted with each person as she worked her way around the tables playing the waitress thing to the hilt. In a Western shirt and blouse with one of Marva's aprons tied around her supple waist, no one could take their eyes off her. Mack was so charmed, his face wore a continual smile.

When she reached Gabe, the fragrance of her skin assailed him. He didn't dare acknowledge her. *He didn't trust himself.*

"Now for the birthday boy," she quipped to everyone's amusement. The boys were loving this! Trust her to come up with another wonderful idea that could be implemented for each teen's birthday.

What he couldn't figure out was where she'd found the time to teach them how to behave at the table! They were models of decorum.

"You may have anything the house offers, sir. Coffee, hot tea, iced tea, orange drink, lemonade or milk."

I'd like to pull you onto my lap and kiss you senseless. That's what I'd like for starters.

"Iced tea, thank you."

"And for your main course?"

He saw his favorite lamb roast tucked in there between the chicken *cordon bleu* and the beef Stroganoff. Everything was in French, more of Stefanie's inspiration.

"The *l'agneau à la menthe, s'il vous plait.*"

"Whoa—Mr. Wainwright!" Gary blurted. "That sounded rad. Whatever you ordered, that's what I'm going to have." Who would guess this from a formerly out of control fourteen-year-old who'd been arrested a dozen times for burglary and auto theft.

Gabe broke out laughing. As his head reared back, his eyes connected with Stefanie's for a moment. She was trying hard to stay in character, but he could tell her shoulders were shaking with silent laughter.

Tonight he was being presented with yet another version of Stefanie Dawson. It frightened him because she seemed to fit in here so naturally.

After working alongside her as they helped deliver Lucky, he conceded that she could do anything, like giving a meal for a bunch of troubled kids who just might make it in life if given half a chance. But she'd be equally at home in the state dining room, gracing a dinner for a group of world leaders trying to find a solution for peace.

Not for the first time since she'd arrived here was he tempted to phone his father and have it confirmed once again from his own lips that Stefanie valued a political marriage at its highest level over true love.

Maybe it was what Gabe needed to hear so he'd be able to stay away from her when she went to work in Kalispell. Hell—his desire for her had grown so intense, he couldn't guarantee that he wouldn't force his way into the old nursery tonight.

The earliest he could call his father was ten. That would make it one o'clock on the East Coast. Gabe had planned to give it a good half year before the two of them talked again. But events beyond Gabe's control had changed the timetable.

During his torturous preoccupation, he didn't realize everyone had finished the main course and was waiting for him to blow out the candles so they could enjoy dessert.

At Gary's urging he got up from his chair and walked over to the cake. Clover followed him. His faithful shadow.

"You have to make a wish," Marva instructed. Stefanie hovered nearby.

A wish...

That was easy.

It was the same wish he'd had when he'd asked Stefanie to dinner on that fateful night.

The wish that she would have answered his question about wanting to be First Lady with, "Only if *you* are my husband. Don't you know I love you so much, I'd live with you in a mud hut if that's what it took to be your wife?"

Her wrong answer had almost destroyed him, just as her unexpected presence at the ranch was going to be his ruination if he didn't do something about it fast.

As soon as he blew out the candles, cake was served. The surprise party Stefanie had planned had not only been an unmitigated success, but it had accomplished a subtle breakthrough between student and staff.

There was an atmosphere of congeniality that hadn't quite been present before. Gabe considered it somewhat of a miracle. When he looked around to thank her, he discovered she'd been cornered by Mack who'd shown a surprising amount of aggressiveness all evening.

Gabe couldn't blame Stefanie for his foreman's behavior. Without any effort on her part, she'd always drawn men to her. If he were being honest, he'd never seen her purposely flirt with another man.

Never once in their marriage had she done anything in or out of his presence that could be construed as provocative behavior.

"Before you all turn in," he spoke up, "let's give a round of applause to Marva and Teri who presented all of us with a night to remember."

While everyone did his bidding, his chief cook went red in the face as she bustled around removing plates from the table. Stefanie was already at the sink doing dishes. Mack stood at her side with a dishcloth in hand to help. Gabe would wait until she was alone before he approached her.

One by one the students and staff filed out of the dining room. He stayed to chat with Marva as they removed tablecloths and put the plaid ones back on in preparation for the next day.

"Gabe?" an anxious female voice called out from the doorway. Everyone's heads turned in that direction.

Madelaine.

With so much going on in his honor, Gabe had almost forgotten about her and Clay. He never noticed that they hadn't come in for dinner. Obviously things were bad. She looked ill.

He hurried over to her. "Where's Clay?"

"I don't know. He wanted to show me his cabin. While we were there I had my talk with him. That's when he dashed out and wouldn't come back. I called and ran after him, but couldn't find him. So I hurried in here to get you."

"He couldn't have gotten very far yet. Go in the living room and wait for me."

"All right."

As she went back through the doors, Mack appeared at his side. "What's the trouble, boss?"

"Clay's disappeared."

"I'll round up the guys and we'll form a search party."

"I'll join you in a minute."

Marva put a hand on his arm. "How can Teri and I help?"

"Take care of Clay's mother."

"Shall I show her to the guest bedroom?"

"That would be fine."

"I'll make up a tray," Stefanie volunteered.

His gaze flashed to hers. "She shouldn't be left alone."

"Don't worry." With those two words she communicated that she understood the reason for his underlying fear. He felt immense relief and gratitude.

Knowing Madelaine would be taken care of, he dashed out of the kitchen to his office with Clover at his heels.

The switch to lock the main gate and set the electric fence could be operated from there. No matter how fast Clay could run, it was still seven miles to the nearest exit. He wouldn't be able to escape.

If he decided to lose himself somewhere on the ranch, it might take a while, but they'd eventually find him. Better them than the police. The judge wouldn't give Clay any more breaks.

Once Gabe had phoned the Wrigleys upstairs to explain the problem so they'd keep an eye out, he took off for the paddock in his Explorer. "Come on, girl. I'm going to need your help."

Clover barked in response, so human at times it was scary.

Okay, Clay Talbot. Where are you? It's time to lay all the cards on the table. I should have done it the day I took you shopping with Stefanie.

* * *

Stefanie placed a cup of hot tea on the tray next to the food. "Marva? I know why Clay ran away, and have a pretty good idea where he went. As soon as I catch up to him, I think I'll be able to fix the problem. If you'll take this to Mrs. Talbot and stay with her, I'll go after him."

"That's fine with me. But why didn't you tell all this to Gabe?"

She expelled a nervous sigh. "Because everything's very complicated right now."

"You're telling me," the cook muttered under her breath.

No doubt the intelligent older woman had divined Stefanie's guilty secret. "I'm going to have to ask you to trust me, Marva."

"I already do."

"Thank you." She hugged her, then ran to the bedroom for her jacket and purse.

Clay loved Gabe and blamed Stefanie for ruining his plans. He wanted to teach both of them a lesson. What better way to put the fear into them than leave the ranch. She had an idea he'd head for Marion and talk one of the tourists at the Branding Iron into giving him a lift to anywhere.

But her plan to head him off met with its first obstacle when she discovered the main gate locked tight. It had never even been closed before! She had no choice but to head back to the main house and find out how to unlock it.

As she was turning around, she heard a noise coming from the back seat of her car. She stepped on the brake and looked over the seat.

"Clay!" It was on the tip of her tongue to ask him how he'd gotten into a locked car. That is until she remembered he'd been caught by the police for these kinds of offenses among others. The little monkey was clever and had decided to hide there until she drove off the property. He might have had a long wait.

On instinct she pushed the electric lock so he couldn't get out, then shut off the engine. Now she had him trapped.

"I know you hate me, but before you do something that will make it impossible for Gabe to help you anymore, you'd better listen to me. Please sit up. It's important."

Her stern voice must have come as something of a surprise because he did her bidding while she reached in the glove compartment for her contact lens case.

"Okay. Now that I can see your eyes, I'd like you to see mine." Throwing caution to the wind, she removed her contact lenses. "Keep looking!"

The admonition wasn't necessary because he appeared glued to what he was seeing. Carefully she took out the bobby pins so she could pull off her wig.

"*Voilà*. You are now gazing at Stefanie Dawson, Gabe's ex-wife."

Silence was golden. She had an idea he was remembering the picture Gabe had told her he'd seen.

Taking advantage of it she plunged ahead. "Instead of going to Europe, I came after him because I love him. If your mother loves him, then she'll have to fight me for him because I won't let him go without a struggle. I've loved him years longer than your mother has, so I have first rights.

"Of course if he returns your mother's love, then there's no contest. But since he hasn't told me anything one way or the other, I'm kind of working in the dark around here.

"When you confided that you were hoping he and your mom would get together, I had to do something quick. Just like you did when you ran out on everyone tonight," she added in effort to get him thinking.

"Gabe told me your mother drinks because she's grieving for your father. I can understand that. He says you've gotten into trouble because you're grieving for your dad, too. I understand that very well.

"As for me, it seems like I've been grieving for Gabe forever. I grieved for him our whole marriage because he didn't ask me to marry him out of love.

"I turned to role-playing instead of alcohol or vandalism. And believe me, I was good at it! So good he never guessed how much I loved him. I'm still playing a role, but I'm sick of it, Clay. So sick of it, I don't know what to do anymore." Her voice shook. "Now it's your turn to talk."

He bowed his head. The next words she heard came out muffled.

"Mom said there was nothing between them but friendship."

Tears stung her eyes.

"I only heard him talk about you once," he admitted grudgingly.

Her heart thudded. "You don't have to tell me."

He lifted his head. She saw a tell-tale mist glazing his eyes. "It might be important. When he mentioned that he was divorced, I asked him why. He said it was because his ex-wife preferred life on the East Coast."

Disappointment shot through her. That was no news to her. "It's what he believes."

"But you came out here wearing that disguise, and he's let you stay. I don't get it."

"He's only given me until the weekend. Then I have to leave."

"That's crazy. When I asked him if you'd seen his ranch, he said it would never happen. Then he told me life didn't always go the way we wanted it to, so it was time we both put the past behind us."

Stefanie stirred restlessly on the seat. What had Gabe meant by that remark? Had he been referring to the fact that he'd had to make a break with his father in order to live the way he wanted?

Or had he meant something else? Something personal to do with their marriage. If Stefanie knew the answer to that question...

But first she needed to help Clay.

"Now that I've told you the truth, despise *me* if you want. Not Gabe. I happen to know he's crazy about you. He brought you all the way from Providence to be with him. He didn't have to do that, and he hasn't done it for any of the other boys.

"Maybe he can't be your father, but he's always been your friend. He always will be if you don't push him away. You see, I know something about him you don't. This ranch represents his lifelong dream. Gabe's here to stay until the day he dies.

"Did you know he has arranged for your mom to get help with her drinking while she's here? He wants the two of you to be a family again. At this point are you prepared to throw everything back in his face?"

One tear, then another trickled down his pale cheeks.

"No," he croaked the word.

"I didn't think so. How about we go back to the ranch? I'll fix it so everything will be all right."

"You'd do that for me?"

"Just watch me!"

She hurriedly put on her wig. When the contact lenses were back in, she started up the car.

Before long they pulled up to the ranch house. Clay followed Stefanie into the foyer. Dr. Wrigley stepped out of the office.

"Clay?"

"It's all right, John," Stefanie forestalled him. "We've been outside talking. Go on upstairs, Clay," she urged the teen. "Your mom's going to be using the guest bedroom while she's here. If Marva's still with her, send her down, will you?"

"Sure." Clay took the stairs two at a time.

The resident psychologist eyed Stefanie a little strangely, but he didn't interfere for which she was grateful. It would come out in therapy soon enough. "I'll inform Gabe so he'll call off the search."

"Thanks, John. I was just going to ask Marva to do it," she said as the older woman started down the stairs.

"Do what?"

"Ask you to phone Gabe with the good news."

"Well, as I always say, all's well that ends well."

"I couldn't agree with you more. Good night, everybody."

Anxious to avoid any discussion, Stefanie locked herself in the bathroom and took a hot shower. After wearing the wig all day, it felt good to wash her hair.

Every night was like déjà vu as she wrapped her head in a towel and poked it out the door to see if the way was clear.

When she could finally turn out the light and get

into bed, she found she was really exhausted. So much effort had been put into the party preparations. Then for Clay to disappear like that...

Thank goodness he *had* run away! The crisis had produced results. Like Gabe had told her, Clay needed to face reality. Tonight he'd been forced to do that. Stefanie felt it was all to the good.

As for her own personal crisis, she finally had answers to one question, which had haunted her since she began the drive across the country. Gabe wasn't in love with Madelaine.

Maybe the two of them had had an affair. It was something Stefanie would never know. But whatever had gone on between them in the way of an amorous nature, if it had gone on, was over.

After the party she'd given him, if he didn't know she was prepared to do anything for him, then she would have to resort to the only option that remained open...cast aside her pride and make an all-out confession.

She would have to pick her time well. Not tonight. Tomorrow night.

Tomorrow night she would steal into his bedroom. If he turned her away...

She buried her face in the pillow. She wouldn't think about that tonight. Tonight she could still dream in possibilities...

"Stefanie?"

Her name was being called from a long distance off. She turned on her back.

"Wake up!"

It sounded like Gabe's voice.

"I'm here."

"I know you are. Get up and unlock the door."

"Don't you have a key?"

"Not for this room."

"Why not?"

"You don't want to know."

He sounded angry. Gabe was always angry about something.

"Don't be cross."

"Stefanie? Have you been drinking?"

When the question registered, she came fully awake.

"Gabe?"

"Contact at last."

She sat up in the cot, pushing the hair out of her eyes. "I-is something wrong?" Her eyes darted to her alarm clock. "It's four in the morning!"

"I've been with a sick calf, but all's well now. Open the door."

This wasn't the night she'd planned to make her confession, but since he was awake, perhaps she should blurt it while she still had the courage.

"I have a better idea. Why don't you go to your bedroom, a-and I'll join you," she stammered. Her heart was pounding so hard it interfered with her breathing.

"If you don't open the door this instant, I'll remove it from the hinges."

He hadn't even heard her! *Or else he had chosen to ignore her offer.*

She'd been given her answer. Her heart seemed to drop from her body to some bottomless pit.

After turning the lock, she got back in the cot. He walked in, slamming the door behind him. The next thing she knew he'd turned on the lamp. There was a vaguely wild look in those green eyes. It made her the slightest bit nervous.

"Why are you looking at me like that?"

His hands went to his hips, dominating the tiny room with his dark, masterful presence. "I was afraid the incident with Clay might have been ugly."

"So you thought I'd resorted to drinking?"

His eyes narrowed on her mouth. "No. Not really. But I had to make sure you were all right."

She struggled for breath. "Have you talked to Clay?"

"No. John Wrigley told me to leave it alone and I agreed with him. Do you mind telling me what happened?"

"Of course not. I figured he wanted to leave the ranch so I went after him in my car. He was hiding in the back seat."

Gabe bit out an epithet. "Why didn't I think of that?"

"Because you weren't the person he'd asked to sneak him out the first time. It's no matter. I needed to be the one to find him. I was able to explain that you cared a lot about him, that even if you couldn't be his father, you would always be his friend. That sort of thing. He seemed to take comfort in those words. Pretty soon he was ready to go back and be with his mother."

He shook his head. "I owe you so much, not only for Clay, but for the surprise party. I loved it. Everyone did. For a little while those troubled boys forgot their problems and lived up to their potential. You're remarkable, Stefanie."

I don't want to be remarkable. There are only three words I want to hear from you. But you'll never say them.

"Mack told me the same thing a little while ago. You've worked your magic on him, just as I thought you would. He asked me what he thought his chances were."

"And I'm sure you told him in no uncertain terms."

His features darkened. "You and I have had this conversation before. He works for me. I can't allow that kind of complication."

"What if I'm interested in him?"

Gabe's mouth twisted unpleasantly. "Don't you think it would be a little cruel to start something you won't be able to finish?"

"He could always visit me in Kalispell."

"Don't try it, Stefanie," he warned.

"Or what?" she blurted, jumping to her feet in anger. The action caused her to brush against him accidentally, sending a current of electricity through her system. The sensation was so pleasurable she never wanted it to stop, but her heart was torn ragged.

Maybe it was a trick of light but she thought she saw a nerve pulsating at the corner of his compelling mouth.

"Why do you care, Gabe? At least Mack is over the death of his wife well enough that he can feel desire again. You should be happy for him."

"Are you insinuating that I don't have those same needs?" His voice sounded like ripping silk.

"I have no idea, do I?"

"Then it's past time you found out!"

His hands went to her arms and whirled her around until she was pressed against the door. A thrill of alarm passed through her body as his head descended. Then his mouth closed over hers.

"Gabe—" she moaned his name, but it was swallowed up in the depth of his passion. A voluptuous shiver passed through her body as his kiss deepened with a hunger she didn't know he possessed.

Her hunger was as great as his. She was so afraid he would pull away, she threw her arms around his neck and molded herself to him without reservation.

They were on fire for each other. His hands and mouth were making her delirious with longing. Everything started to spiral out of control.

"I have needs, Stefanie. I want you more than you know," he murmured huskily against her throat. "You have to let me love you, but not here, not on that cot." His breathing was as shallow as hers.

"Your room then?" she cried, feverishly covering his eyes, nose and mouth with kisses.

He lifted his head and ran his hands through her hair. "No—I can afford to take some time off. We'll drive to Marion and get a room. Hurry and dress, then meet me at the car."

She was in such a euphoric daze, it took her a minute to realize he meant for them to go to the Branding Iron.

After waiting years for this moment, he wanted to take her to a cheap motel? It didn't make sense.

In Stefanie's mind unmarried people sneaking out to a motel seemed illicit, clandestine.

A motel was a place a man took a woman when he didn't want to be seen with her anywhere else. A place to carry on a relationship he couldn't be proud of in public.

To her, it meant a one-night stand.

Passion without enduring love.

Stefanie hadn't been wrong about Gabe wanting her. To prove it to herself, she'd baited him just now to get the reaction she'd desired.

But it had backfired on her with heartbreaking results because he never said the words.

No matter his reasons for wanting to take her to a secret rendezvous away from the ranch, none of them were good enough for her to consider it.

He'd walked away from their marriage without touching her. The second that March 28 had rolled around, he'd reached for his freedom with both hands.

Now that she was on the premises, why not enjoy a tawdry affair with his ex-wife until her departure? *Dear God.* She thought she'd known pain before...

He buried his face in her hair. "Why aren't you saying anything?"

"Because I never intended for things to go this far." Her whole body was shaking. "Your comment about Mack made me angry, so I foolishly retaliated. But all I managed to do was bring out the anger in you."

His hands tightened on her shoulders. "You think I kissed you in anger?" he whispered fiercely.

"I know you did. But it doesn't matter because I don't intend to provoke you again. A few more days and I'll be gone."

She pulled completely away from him. "I'm sorrier than you that I came out to Montana. Everything that's happened has been my fault. When you left Newport, we parted on amicable terms. I'd like to get back on that same footing again before I leave.

"Forgive me, Gabe." She extended her hand. "Friends?"

In the dim light, his face seemed to have lost color. He ignored the gesture.

"After what happened between us just now, you really believe we can go back to being friends?"

"Of course. It's the civilized thing to do."

One black brow dipped sardonically. "That's something a politician would say. You've learned your craft better than anyone I know. But why not?" His smile was wintry. "My father was the master teacher. I can see I've been cruel in enforcing that six-month restriction.

"As a gesture of goodwill, I'm going to rescind our contract. When I go upstairs, I'll phone both sets of parents and invite them out for an official tour of the ranch. While they're here I'll tell them the truth about our marriage. When they're ready to leave, you can fly back with them."

Stefanie was horrified.

The senator's words rang in her ears. *I expect you to bring my son to his senses. I want him home by the end of the week.* She got this suffocating feeling in her chest.

"I—I don't understand. I thought you needed time."

"So did I. But now that I've settled in, there's no point in waiting. It'll be a circus no matter when they're told. For everyone concerned, it's best we get it over with."

"No, Gabe!" His words filled her with absolute panic. If he found out she'd already told their parents everything, he'd never forgive her.

"Why not?" he demanded. His eyes scorched her face. To her horror she realized he could sense her guilt.

"B-because it *won't* be better!" she cried out. "The press will be alerted and plant their cameras outside the fences to watch for any sign of you. The students don't need that kind of publicity. It'll disrupt their school schedule. Clay and his mother are just barely making progress. You can't do that to them!

"Think of the stockmen who will be harassed. Every time Mack goes to town, someone will dog his footsteps wanting information. Poor Marva will be afraid to show her face. You *have* to give yourself more time before you and your ranch are plastered all over the front page of every major newspaper in the country!

"Your original plan for us to bow out of the scene for six months makes perfect sense, Gabe. Be honest with me—the only reason you're thinking of changing the timetable is because of *me!* I trespassed on your private life.

"Promise me you won't let what I've done destroy everything. Please—you've put something together here that's so magnificent, so worthy and wonderful, I can't find the words. The great good you're going to accomplish for hundreds of boys over a lifetime is incalculable.

"I couldn't bear it if something went wrong at this early stage because of my interference."

Scalding tears spilled from her eyes and down her cheeks. "I'm begging you—" Her voice throbbed. "On the strength of the marriage contract we both signed, don't do anything to jeopardize it yet."

"That contract be damned!"

Gabe locked the office door behind him. He needed a drink fast. Unfortunately he'd made it a rule not to keep hard liquor on the premises. *Another mistake.*

He unlocked his minifridge where he kept a variety of drinks for the occasional one-on-one with a student or staff member. After popping open a beer, he flung himself into the leather swivel chair and drained it.

Gabe needed illumination.

Beer couldn't perform the required miracle. It couldn't blunt the worst of the pain. It wouldn't even come close. All it accomplished was to give him something physical to do while he tried to make sense of this night.

The thing that had happened in Stefanie's bedroom had shaken him to the foundations. She'd kissed him in raw passion. In fact she'd done a lot more than that. For one fantastic moment he'd felt their souls as well as their bodies commune in a way that transcended all other experiences in life.

Then like a flash of lightning, the beautiful glowing woman who'd come alive in his arms suddenly turned off!

It wasn't natural. A person didn't behave like that without a reason.

Not once during their marriage, or while she'd been on the ranch, had she given him cause to believe she was the kind of woman who derived a thrill from luring a man to a line she had no intention of crossing.

In fact the adorable Ms. Jones he'd rescued in the storm had convinced him she enjoyed the Montana lifestyle, maybe even loved it. There'd been moments when he could have sworn her feelings for him matched his in intensity. A few minutes ago he'd been offered proof of that desire. His body still throbbed from her rapturous response.

Then out of nowhere she'd retreated. Emotionally as well as physically.

He crushed the empty can in his hand and tossed it.

Why would she pull away from him like that when he could still see her eyes blazing a hot blue for him?

She'd grown frantic when he'd told her he was going to invite their parents to the ranch. Instead of her being relieved he was willing to abrogate their contract so she could return to Newport right away, she begged him not to change the terms.

In the space of a heartbeat, he'd watched the burning desire in those eyes change to fear.

Something was wrong. She'd begged him not to call his father. That in itself made Gabe suspicious.

He glanced at his watch. It would be after eight on the East Coast. Under the circumstances, this was the best time to find his parents home. Acquainted with the madness of an elected congressman's schedule, another few hours and Gabe might not be so lucky.

He'd follow with a call to Stefanie's parents.

There was a private number utilized by the family so they could always reach his father. Gabe hadn't used it in months. Without hesitation he picked up the receiver and punched the digits.

CHAPTER NINE

DRESSED for riding, Stefanie crept down the hall to the kitchen. Once she'd grabbed some food and drinks from the fridge, she tiptoed to the back door. Being as quiet as she could, she slipped outside and headed for the barn.

The sun hadn't come up over the horizon yet, but there was enough light to see her way. She'd come to love early morning on the ranch. Despite her pain, there was a tranquil beauty that fed her soul.

Gabe was probably on the phone to his parents right now. She didn't want to be anywhere around when he learned she was the reason why all his secrets had been exposed. What he didn't know was that once he'd driven off on the morning of their divorce, she couldn't bear living the lie a moment longer.

It wasn't a matter of his not forgiving her. That was to be expected. What she couldn't bear to see was the disappointment in his eyes because he'd lost trust in her.

If she didn't return to the ranch until evening, hopefully by then he would have gotten over his initial anger. Maybe at that point she could explain why she'd gone behind his back in the first place.

It wouldn't change anything. But at least he'd know that everything she'd done since she'd met him had been because she was in love with him. At least then he would have an understanding of her motives and not despise her too much.

"Teri?"

She'd been so intent on her thoughts of Gabe, she hadn't seen anyone else coming.

"Good morning, Mack."

He opened the barn door for her. "What are you doing up this early? I told you while we were washing the dishes—after all the preparations you did for the boss's birthday party last night—I didn't want you to come in to work this morning."

"I know, and I appreciate it. Actually I woke up early to take a ride. I'd like to check on one of the new calves."

A smile lit up Mack's eyes. "You mean Lucky?"

Apparently he and Gabe shared a great deal. "I see there are no secrets around here."

"Not too many," was his mysterious response. "I'm headed in that direction myself. Want some company?"

She'd promised Gabe she wouldn't encourage Mack, but this was one time she feared that if she turned the foreman down, it might hurt his feelings. That was the last thing she wanted to do.

"I'd like it a lot."

"Good."

He insisted on helping her. They bridled and saddled Molly with dispatch.

"I've got this sack of food. Will it be all right if I put it in one of the saddlebags?"

"Sure. I'll sling it on Molly."

They walked her horse to the paddock where his was saddled. He gave orders to a half-dozen stockmen getting ready for the day, then the two of them rode out.

More confident in the saddle than before, Stefanie set a fast pace, anxious to get as far away from the ranch as possible in the shortest amount of time. Mack kept even with her. At one point he asked her why she was in such a big hurry.

"I noticed all those clouds. They're moving toward us. I'd like to reach the meadow before it decides to rain."

He glanced at the sky. "It just might do that, but it won't happen till late in the day. We've got a nice level stretch through here. Let's give the horses their head."

She fastened the tie under her chin. "You're on!"

Mack took off like a torpedo. She urged Molly to a gallop. It was exhilarating to fly over the ground with the wind zinging past her ears, bending back the rim of her cowboy hat.

He was waiting for her when she came around the big bend in the river she remembered from before. The herd could be seen in the distance. She laughed as she rode up to him.

"That was wonderful. Especially watching you ride. Smooth as glass, and effortless. You remind me of a cowboy out of a Charles Russell painting. I guess you'd have to be born out here to learn how to ride the way you do."

His eyes glinted with a mixture of pleasure and admiration. "You're doing fine, Teri."

"Mr. Wainwright probably pays you to say things like that. Keep the staff happy."

Oddly enough Mack's expression sobered. "Not at all." He looked around, leaning on the horn.

"Well, this is where we part company. When I've repaired some fencing, I'll head back this way to check on you."

"Thank you, but I'm sure I'll be fine."

He waved farewell and headed uphill into the forest. She watched until she couldn't see him anymore, then she cantered toward the cows. Without Gabe here, she didn't feel quite as brave as before. The animals seemed more restless. Perhaps they were sensitive to a change in the weather.

Deciding not to penetrate the herd, she made a broad circle around them. There were fifteen mothers with new babies. From this distance Stefanie couldn't pick out Lucky.

Her plan to sit and watch him hadn't worked out. It would be a long time before evening. Since she wasn't hungry yet, she decided to ride on.

The phone rang three times before Gabe heard a click.

"Yes?"

His father's voice always sounded gruff when he'd been asleep. But Gabe heard something else in it just now, as if he feared bad news. Paranoia was the bedfellow of the dedicated politician.

"Hello, Dad."

After an exaggerated silence, "Thank God!"

Almost simultaneously Gabe could hear his mother making joyful noises in the background.

"You sound relieved. I told you in my letter I'd stay in touch with you."

"Forget that absurdity. I knew Stefanie wouldn't let me down. But I expected that daughter-in-law of mine to have brought you home by last weekend at the latest!''

Gabe sat forward in the chair, puzzled by his father's comments. ''As usual it sounds like you know more about my wife's agenda than I do.''

''Look, son. Let's not beat around the bush. She told us everything, and we've kept quiet. But you can never keep the lid on these things very long, so come on home. Your mom and I are prepared to forget any of this foolishness ever happened.''

He shot to his feet, unable to contain his pain in a seated position. ''What do you mean Stefanie told you everything?''

''Don't use that tone with me. You have no right to be angry with either of us. No right at all. After what you did to her, we're lucky Grant isn't suing us for every dime we've got.''

Livid, Gabe blurted, ''Why would Stefanie's father want to do that?''

''Between you and me, a man can be forgiven most anything except taking advantage of another man's daughter. Dammit, Gabriel— Surely if you needed a front, you could have come up with something better than a marriage of convenience! Do you have any idea how that sounds?

''I don't care if you don't love her. You need to get home and make a real marriage with her.''

A shudder rocked Gabe's body.

All this time Stefanie had been on a secret mission for his father… Everything she'd said and done since Gabe had left Newport had been a lie. Only in his case, the ex-husband had been the last person to know.

"Are you listening, son? Where in the hell are you, and what do you think you're doing?"

The time for complete honesty had come. Without mincing words, Gabe explained about the ranch. He repeated what he'd told Stefanie about his reasons for settling here.

"I'm afraid any plans to make it to the White House are out, Dad. But then that was your dream for me and Stefanie. I can tell you right now, it's never going to happen. However there's always hope for her. She's a free agent. There's nothing to stop her from marrying a man who'll take her there."

"Gabe—son—bring her back home and at least make a marriage with her."

"I live here now, Dad."

"But she doesn't want another man."

"The hell she doesn't!" Gabe was still reeling from her rejection of him half an hour ago. "You've been her mentor all along. Surely you can find her a man with the right stuff. As you've so often told me, she can't wait to be the First Lady."

His father chuckled nervously, which was totally unlike him. "Gabriel—you know your old dad. I only said that to get you thinking."

"Come again?"

"It's no secret I wanted the two of you to get together."

He gripped the receiver tighter. "So what are you saying exactly?" When his father didn't answer right away Gabe blurted, "Are you telling me you *lied* about that?"

"At the time it seemed harmless," his father answered quietly.

Then that meant—

Gabe's heart almost exploded out of its chest cavity.

"I've got to go, Dad."

"Wait— Son— Tell Stefanie I apologize for being so hard on her."

What else had his father done he didn't know about? Only Stefanie had the answers.

"Gabe, darling?" His mother must have been listening the whole time. "Call again soon. We love you."

"We do," was his father's muffled rejoinder.

"I love you, too."

He hung up the receiver with an excitement he couldn't control. Finally he was going to have the confrontation with Stefanie that had been destined for what seemed like a lifetime...

Before he did anything else, he checked her bedroom on the off chance that she'd slept in. Disappointed when he found the nursery empty, he decided it was for the best. After being up all night he needed to shower and shave.

Twenty minutes later he and Clover hurried down to the kitchen. Marva served him breakfast. Apparently she hadn't seen Teri and didn't expect her until the afternoon. That meant Stefanie was hard at work in the barn. He took off in that direction.

"Hi, Mr. Wainwright!"

"David? How's it coming?"

"Really good, sir."

"Glad to hear it." He chatted with a couple of the boys mucking out the stalls. There was a definite improvement in their mood. The party last night had done wonders for morale. "You're doing a fine job."

He walked back outside where Mack's assistant

was getting ready to shoe one of the horses. "Good morning, Will."

"Gabe? Heard you had yourself some birthday party last night."

"It came as a total surprise. I'd like to thank Ms. Jones since she was in on the planning end."

"I haven't seen her this morning."

He frowned. "What about Mack?"

"Some cows got out and strayed up the blue ridge. He took off to repair the fence. I don't expect him back till late."

"Thanks, Will."

Maybe John Wrigley had asked Stefanie to sit in on a session with Clay and his mother this morning. She couldn't have left the ranch because he hadn't unlocked the main gate yet.

Growing impatient, his gaze swerved to the paddock. He could account for every horse, but there was no sign of Molly. Galvanized into action, he returned to the barn. The mare wasn't in her stall!

When Gabe had walked out on Stefanie earlier this morning, he'd left her in a distressed state. There was no other word for it. He'd never seen her so utterly devastated. But his own agony had propelled him out of the room before he lost total control. Evidently she'd turned to riding to deal with her turmoil.

Mack was always up early. Surely he would have seen her at the barn.

Gabe whipped out his cell phone to call his foreman. To his relief he didn't have to wait too long to hear the click.

"This is Mack."

"Mack? It's Gabe. Did you see Teri this morning? Molly's gone."

"As a matter of fact she rode with me as far as the river pasture. She wanted to check up on Lucky. I told her I'd swing by there again on my way back later. Is everything okay, boss?"

A heaving sigh escaped. "It is now. Thanks, Mack. I'll be headed that way in a minute. Stay in touch."

He put his phone away and dashed out of the barn. "Will? If anyone asks, I've gone to the river pasture."

The older stockman nodded.

While Gabe saddled Caesar, he noticed thunderheads building. There would be fireworks by late afternoon.

As imperative as it was that he get the truth out of Stefanie, his first priority had to be her safety. If he rode hard, he could have her back home before the storm hit. Then he'd take her someplace private and...

Dear God. He couldn't think beyond getting her alone, holding her, loving her like he'd done for those brief minutes in her bedroom this morning.

Those memories were all that sustained him as he made the ride to the meadow in record time. But his heart dropped like a stone when he galloped close to the herd and couldn't find her.

He contacted Mack on the cell phone once more. "There's no sign of Teri."

"Maybe she got nervous and decided to join me. I'll ride back the way I came and meet you halfway."

His foreman's plan made good sense. "See you soon."

But when they met each other a half hour later without either one of them having found her, Gabe felt a pit the size of a crater in his gut. The wind had started to pick up. She would notice the drop in temperature.

"I've got to find her, Mack." His lids closed tightly. "After all we've been through, if anything were to happen to Stefanie before I could tell her how I feel..."

"Boss— I know we're talking about Teri, but just now you called her Stefanie."

Gabe eyed his foreman. "Stefanie's my ex-wife."

"That explains it," Mack murmured. "I never saw a man so crazy about a woman in my life! What in the hell are you doing letting her sleep alone every night?"

"There are things you don't know."

"I don't need to know them," he retorted. "I don't care what caused the divorce. The chemistry's there. It's powerful. I'd give anything to have my wife back!"

"Don't you know how lucky you are to be loved by a woman like Stefanie? She worships the ground you walk on."

"I want to believe that, Mack." His voice shook. "That's why I have to find her. I need to hear her say those words."

"She's around here somewhere licking her wounds."

"What do you mean?"

"I rode with her this morning. She had all the signs of a brokenhearted woman. We'll find her, boss. I already alerted the hands. They're making a sweep now. Where do you want to look?"

"The other night we stayed at the old fire watchtower. I told her that's where the stockmen go if they need shelter. Maybe she got so frightened, she headed there. I pray she's not lost. I'm going to search that area first.''

''I'll swing around the other way.''

''Mack—thanks for being my friend.''

''Ditto. By the way, it's nice to be back in your good graces again.''

Gabe had turned his horse to get going, but he stopped long enough to look over his shoulder at Mack. ''What do you mean?''

''For a man who always seems to have everything under control, you're downright scary when you're jealous.''

From the vantage point of the fire tower porch, Stefanie watched the cloudburst do its worst. She could have made it back to the ranch before the storm broke. But knowing Gabe would already have talked to his parents, her fear of his reaction was so great, she'd chosen to hide from him a little longer.

To her shame she hadn't considered anyone else when she'd made that rash decision. Last night Clay had run off and Gabe had gone looking for him. Tonight he would be looking for *her*, compounding a never-ending, explosive situation between them. Guilt smote her when she realized he would have summoned every hand on the ranch to comb the property for signs of her.

Rather than the violence of the elements, it was his state of mind that had her body trembling with fear. If her cell phone batteries hadn't died on her, she would have phoned the main house to let them know she was all right.

Intermittent sheet lightning, punctuated by thunder, illuminated the inside of the tower. Between episodes, the darkness would have been daunting if not for the light from the butane lantern. She set it next to the cot while she made dinner out of the rest of the food she'd brought.

Molly was tied under a huge cluster of pines where Stefanie hoped the horse would stay the driest. Lightning struck trees, so it was probably the wrong place to put her, but she couldn't just let the horse stand in the open and take the full brunt of the rain.

If Stefanie were a more experienced outdoorswoman, *a more experienced anything,* she would head back to the ranch as soon as the storm passed over.

En route she might even bump into some stockmen who would not only be out looking for her, but were taking shifts through the night to help with problem deliveries of the new spring calves.

On the other hand, it was possible she wouldn't see anyone in the darkness. If she got lost, she could get into serious trouble. It would be better to stay here and start out tomorrow under the clear sky of day.

After she finished eating, she sat huddled in the middle of the cot with the blankets drawn around her. She used another blanket to try to dry her hair.

A strong gust of wind had blown her hat away before the downpour began. By the time she'd climbed the ladder, her wig was shot. It lay on the floor in a dark, sodden heap.

That was the way she felt right now. All washed-up and black with despair.

She'd never thought beyond Gabe. It hadn't been

a part of her consciousness to consider existence without him.

Get used to it, Stefanie. This is the way it's going to be from now on.

While he attempted to quell the furious pounding of his heart, Gabe studied Stefanie from the doorway of the tower.

Once he'd spotted Molly beneath the pines, the frantic beat should have subsided out of relief that he'd found her. But such wasn't the case.

Now that she was within touching distance, his adrenaline had gone haywire. Too much energy suppressed for too long couldn't be held back any longer.

Huddled under the blankets with the thunder rolling in, it was little wonder she hadn't heard him climb the ladder. No matter how he announced his presence, it was going to frighten her.

"Stefanie?"

At the sound of his voice she scrambled off the cot, leaving the blankets in a pile. With her glorious blond hair in seductive disarray and her damp shirt and jeans molded to her breathtaking body, he didn't know where to look first.

Every inch of her reached out to him, so vital and alive he wanted to absorb her essence into his being where she would live forever.

He moved closer, obeying the siren call of those eyes more beguiling than blue flame. A hand went out, as if to hold him off. She took a step backward.

"Y-you don't need to say a word, Gabe. I know what I've done. The rain is letting up. If we leave for the ranch now, I'll get in my car and go away for good. I swear it.''

Gabe hadn't been able to get to the tower fast enough. But now that he'd found her and could see that she wasn't injured or ill, a great calm had come over him. His body relaxed. She was hoping for a quick retreat. She obviously didn't understand the rules of war.

"There was a time not too long ago when I trusted you with my life, Stefanie. But your presence at the ranch after I arrived, combined with certain information my father brought to light at four this morning, has led me to believe your oath is about as enduring as a garment in a hot furnace.''

He tossed his hat aside, then removed his gloves and jacket.

"Don't say that!'' she cried out, her eyes swimming in liquid. "I can explain everything. There were compelling reasons why I followed you out here.''

"I've already heard them, so let's not waste time covering the same ground again.''

He'd always found those reasons suspect. Now was the time to wring every ounce of truth from her. The trouble was, he wanted to touch her so badly, he had to keep his arms folded.

"Why don't you start at the point where I drove away in the limo and you ran straight to my father to receive further instructions.''

A hand fluttered to her throat. "It wasn't like that, Gabe.''

"Then enlighten me.''

While he waited breathlessly for her next explanation, he reached for the air mattresses and started to fill them using an old bicycle pump.

She followed him. "You seem to have this idea that your father and I were in league together in some great conspiracy."

His head reared back. "Shall I tell you how it looked from my vantage point? Throughout the year leading up to our marriage, you two were so tight, I suspected you of having an affair."

He saw her throat working. "You don't really mean that." She sounded aghast. When he didn't say anything else, she cried, "You *do* mean it. *Gabe*—"

She sounded close to hysterics as she knelt by him, clutching his arm. "I swear nothing could be further from the truth!"

Recalling those gut-wrenching suspicions brought back in full force the excruciating pain he thought he'd buried long ago.

"You have a poor memory, Stefanie. Didn't we just establish that your word hasn't necessarily been your bond?"

The peaches and cream color drained out of her face, making her beauty more ethereal. "You have it all wrong," her voice trembled. "Totally and completely wrong."

He wanted to believe her, but the old demons were still driving him. "You mean he was hoping for an affair with you, but he was only a senator, and you were playing for higher stakes?"

CHAPTER TEN

"Much higher stakes," she whispered.

A bleak look entered his eyes. "That's probably the first honest thing you've ever said to me."

"Gabe—" She found his hand and grasped it in both of hers. "I can't remember a time when I didn't love you with all my heart. Do you know after I went to work for your father, I started keeping a scrapbook on you?"

Gabe pulled his hand away and rose to his full, intimidating height. "Don't lie to me, Stefanie."

Stunned by his reaction because so much damage had been done, she got to her feet. "I'm not lying, darling."

Her endearment caused him to pale. She refused to let him put distance between them. Before this night was over she was determined he would learn how much he was loved.

"When we get back to the ranch, I'll show it to you. It's so full I really need to start another one. The magazines and newspapers were always full of stories about you. Every week I cut out a new clipping to add to my precious collection."

She saw him rub the back of his neck absently. It meant he was listening.

"You'll probably laugh when I tell you that the day I met you on your father's yacht, I made up my mind that one day when I was all grown up, I was going to marry you."

Silence followed her confession. Maybe she was starting to get through to him. He hadn't accused her of lying to him this time.

"After I'd been working for your father for a while, I asked Daddy why the last Wainwright son had stayed a bachelor. He said you were probably still single because you had a brilliant political future ahead of you. Any man rumored to be a future candidate for president of the U.S. would choose his wife more carefully than most men."

Gabe searched her eyes. "I had no idea."

"I asked him if he thought I could be that woman. Like a loving father, he told me any man would be very lucky to get me for a wife. It was sweet of him, but it wasn't the answer I was looking for.

"I begged him to be serious for a minute. What did I need to do to attract *you?*

"He studied me for a minute, then he said, 'You're thirteen years younger than he is. That's all right as long as you can be his intellectual and emotional helpmate.'

"I took what he said to heart, but to my dismay I rarely saw you around campaign headquarters. It seemed your brothers were much more involved in politics than you were. I—I was crushed."

Gabe shook his head, as if he still couldn't believe what he was hearing.

"When your father's assistant came down with bronchitis and had to take time off, I was asked to be her replacement. It was a great opportunity, but deep down I couldn't help hoping I would get to see more of you.

"He warned me I would have to work all hours of the day and night. I assured him that was fine.

Your father seemed pleased with that answer. I worked hard and received my reward when his assistant came back and he gave her another position instead.

"Your father and I worked well together. That made me proud, but he never knew my love for you had a lot to do with my job satisfaction. Little by little he confided private things to me.

"Early on I learned how much he loved you, what great hopes he had for his youngest son to sit in the White House one day. All I knew was that I loved you, too. It was the love affair over *you* that bonded your father and me. Nothing else.

"Whatever he wanted for you, I wanted it, too. I tried so hard to get you to really notice me, but nothing seemed to work. That afternoon I found you on the shore cleaning fish I thought, 'He's going to ask me to stay with him tonight.'

"But you didn't—" her voice caught "—I waited to hear the words. They never came.

"Those three weeks before your surprise phone call were the blackest I had ever known. Then I heard your voice on the line asking me to dinner. It was as if sunshine filled my universe once more.

"I remembered what my father had said. A man who planned on being president of the U.S. would be very careful when it came to choosing a wife. More than anything in the world, I wanted to be that woman."

Gabe's sharp intake of breath resounded in the tower. "Let's talk about that night. I asked you if it was true what my father said, that you hoped to be First Lady one day. Do you remember what you answered?"

"Yes!" she cried.

"I'd like to hear it again."

"I said, 'Isn't it every woman's dream?'"

His hands balled into fists. "This morning on the phone, my father admitted that you never told him any such thing. Stefanie—" His voice sounded as if it was coming from some underground cavern. "If you loved me as much as you say you did, and you knew he'd lied, why did you allow me to go on thinking something that wasn't true?"

She groaned. "Haven't you listened to anything I've been telling you? It was because I thought it was the answer *you* wanted to hear!"

"Lord."

"Don't you see, darling? You never told me the whole idea of running for president was abhorrent to you. You never told anybody. Even my parents thought it was a foregone conclusion. Naturally I had no clue.

"I loved you, Gabe. When you asked me that question, I thought you were leading up to a marriage proposal. At that point I would have said or done anything to be your wife. *Anything!*"

An angry laugh of self-abnegation escaped her lips. "When you asked for no more lies, you got a lot more than you bargained for." Her confession had probably revolted him.

"I still haven't heard everything." His voice sounded strange. Thick.

"Obviously you told the family the truth. I want the details. What did my father mean when he told me he knew you wouldn't let him down?"

She took a deep breath. "On the day you left, I asked our parents to meet me at the yacht club for dinner. They thought I was going to tell them we were having a baby.

"When they heard the truth, both our fathers were furious, but for different reasons. Your dad was furious with me for not telling him about our bogus marriage sooner. He demanded to know where you'd gone.

"I told him I didn't have any idea, but that I was going to find out because I couldn't live without you. As I was leaving the club, he ordered me to bring you home by the weekend. Little did he know I had absolutely no influence over you.

"I guess when you phoned him, he thought I had met with some success. I'm pretty sure it shocked your father to find out my loyalty had always been to you."

"I'm sure it did," Gabe murmured, but he didn't sound quite as fierce as before. "For what it's worth, he asked me to tell you he apologized for being so hard on you."

She averted her eyes. "I'm glad. I love your parents, Gabe. They've been wonderful to me. That's why it didn't seem fair to let them go on thinking one thing w-when we'd just divorced."

While she'd been talking, he'd put the mattresses on the floor side by side. "I have news for you, sweetheart. We're still married."

Her eyes widened. "I don't understand. I saw the document. I signed it!"

"That was the contract. I tore it up." He tossed some pillows on the mattresses with the blankets. "Our marriage is still binding. Therefore your legal name will continue to be Wainwright, and it's going to stay that way for the duration.

"Now—I don't know about you, but it's been a long day and night. Is there anything else you have to do before I turn off the lantern?"

Shock made her slow on the uptake. The light went out, enclosing them in the intimacy of darkness. She could tell he was removing his boots.

"I can hear your teeth chattering, Stefanie. Come to bed."

"That's all right. You need sleep. I'm not tired yet. I'll just get me some more bl—"

But the rest of the word never came out because two strong hands grasped her shoulders.

"Your clothes are still damp. You need to get out of them." His hand went to the top button of her blouse.

Tremor after tremor shook her body. "Gabe?"

He kissed her lips quiet. "I gave you time to come clean about your lies. Now it's my turn for confession. We're going to need all night.

"The truth is, I've been in love with you for so long, I can't think straight anymore. Tonight I'm going to make you my true wife the way I ached to do months ago. Perhaps by morning you'll begin to have some idea of what you mean to me."

He drew her down on the mattress. She moved into his arms with an eagerness that would cause her to blush later when she thought about it. Their mouths and bodies found each other and clung.

Stefanie needed no proof that Gabe was starving for her. The freedom to love him at last transcended any dreams. She didn't know love could be this powerful and all-encompassing.

As he kissed her with a refined savagery that took her breath, she realized this was her husband worshipping her. Only now was she beginning to comprehend how glorious it was to be a woman.

Sated from hours of lovemaking, they had just fallen asleep when noisy birdsong outside the tower caused Stefanie to stir. She opened her eyes. The sky had a lavender-blue cast. It was morning already!

Gabe had promised they would talk, but once he'd started kissing her, coherent thought had ceased for either of them. Throughout the night he'd made her feel immortal. Now she was awake again, hungry for him and full of questions.

She leaned over his magnificent body and started to kiss his mouth, making each foray a little longer and deeper until he was moving and breathing with her. Groaning his need, they repeated the timeless ritual that had united soul and body throughout the night.

Much later she whispered against his neck, "Tell me something—"

"That I love you?" he whispered into her silky hair. "That I think you're the most adorable, kind-hearted, sensitive, courageous, exciting woman a man was ever blessed to have for his wife?"

"That'll do for starters." She crushed him to her. "I just want to know why you wanted to take me to a motel instead of your bedroom?"

His hand caressed her hip. "There are other families living upstairs. I wanted to make love to my wife someplace private for our first time. Of course now that we have a perfect understanding between us, I know how your mind works. You thought I was propositioning you."

"That's exactly what I thought."

His chuckle delighted her. "My love, I plan to proposition you endlessly from here on out and don't expect another rejection like that again. I couldn't take it," he admitted on a note that revealed his vulnerability.

"I love you too much for that, Gabe." She covered his face in kisses. "When did you know you loved me?"

His chest rose and fell deeply. "I'm not sure of the exact moment. The first time I saw you on the yacht, I thought you were the most beautiful creature I had ever seen."

She gasped. "I thought the same thing about you."

"Men aren't beautiful."

"*You* are."

He crushed her in his arms.

"That was over ten years ago." She groaned. "I've loved you for so long."

Gabe's thoughts flew back in time. He'd just turned twenty-six, a recent graduate of Harvard law school and already set up in a prestigious Newport law firm.

"You were very young, darling, but I saw the promise of the woman in the girl. Years later at campaign headquarters, I caught sight of a pair of heavenly blue eyes and realized my prediction had come true. If anything you'd turned out to be even more breathtaking than I had first envisioned."

Stefanie burrowed into his neck. "I wish I'd known."

"You had charm, intelligence. Your charisma infected everyone, especially my father. I began watching you, the way you handled him. In many ways he's a hard man, but you brought out a nicer side of him. At first I found myself curious, then envious, then jealous to the point of rage.''

''Oh, Gabe—I'm so sorry.''

He kissed her long and hard.

''You have nothing to apologize for. I'd fallen in love with you, and was too blinded by my emotions to see that both of you were innocent. The question I asked you at dinner was most definitely a test. I wanted you to answer, 'No. My only desire is to be your wife. Period.'

''When I didn't elicit the response I desired, I came up with that marriage of convenience. One way or the other, I was going to have you!''

Her eyes glistened like blue gemstones. ''I should have said the words that were in my heart. What a fool I was.''

''No more than I. We've wasted far too much time. When I found you in the snow and discovered you were Teri Jones, I swear my heart leaped for joy.''

She moaned in remembrance of that moment. ''I must have been the last person to know it.''

He cupped her face in his hands, trapping her gaze. ''On the drive out to the ranch with Clay, I felt I was in mourning. Even if you'd followed through with the plans to travel, I don't think I could have stayed away from you very long.

''In my gut I knew that at some point I would have come for you. During our marriage you'd been a torment to me. You were in my blood, darling. If I couldn't have you, I didn't want anyone else.''

Stefanie wrapped her arms around him. ''I'm here to stay, Gabe. If you want to know the truth, I would

have made a horrible First Lady. I hate the time politicians have to be away their loved ones.

"Don't get me wrong. I admire men like our fathers. Someone has to do the work and pay the price.
But I'm so thankful it's not you."

A smile broke out on his handsome face. "You
really mean that, don't you?"

"As I told you before, I hope the first of our children, however many are sent to us, is born nine
months from today. A child needs his father every
day, not just once a month and sometimes on holi-
days.

"The Wainwright children in this family are going
to be around their father on a constant basis. You
can't ask for more happiness than that."

"I agree, as long as you're their mother."

He slid a possessive hand across her stomach. "If
that miracle has already happened, we need to build
another cabin on the property to house this brood of
ours."

"I'm way ahead of you. Let's ask your brother
Richard if he wants to buy the house in Newport. It
was our first house together, and it was beautiful,
but—"

"But it was never our home." He could read her
mind.

"No. As far as I'm concerned, this fire watchtower
is *home*."

Gabe chewed on one delicate earlobe. "Our special place."

"Our children will love it."

"Their father already loves it. It was here every
desire of his heart was fulfilled."

"Hey, pardner—" Her eyes twinkled wickedly.

"You sound as if this roundup is all over. I have news for you, birthday boy. This is just the beginning. It's time you got to work making the little woman happy all over again. You can't be shirking your duties at this stage. No siree."

A burst of deep male laughter resounded well beyond the tower.

The two stockmen searching for strays paused to listen.

"That sounds like the boss."

"Yup."

"I never heard him laugh like that before."

"Nope."

"He sure sounds happy."

"Yup."

THE AUSTRALIANS

MEN WHO TURN YOUR WHOLE WORLD UPSIDE DOWN!

Look out for novels about the Wonder from Down Under—where spirited women win the hearts of Australia's most eligible men.

Harlequin Romance®:

OUTBACK WITH THE BOSS
Barbara Hannay (September, #3670)

MASTER OF MARAMBA
Margaret Way (October, #3671)

OUTBACK FIRE
Margaret Way (December, #3678)

Harlequin Presents®:

A QUESTION OF MARRIAGE
Lindsay Armstrong (October, #2208)

FUGITIVE BRIDE
Miranda Lee (November, #2212)

Available wherever Harlequin books are sold.

HARLEQUIN®
Makes any time special®

If you enjoyed what you just read,
then we've got an offer you can't resist!

Take 2 bestselling love stories FREE!

Plus get a FREE surprise gift!

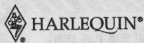

Harlequin truly does make any time special. . . . This year we are celebrating weddings in style!

To help us celebrate, we want you to tell us how wearing the Harlequin wedding gown will make your wedding day special. As the grand prize, Harlequin will offer one lucky bride the chance to **"Walk Down the Aisle"** in the Harlequin wedding gown!

There's more...

For her honeymoon, she and her groom will spend five nights at the **Hyatt Regency Maui.** As part of this five-night honeymoon at the hotel renowned for its romantic attractions, the couple will enjoy a candlelit dinner for two in Swan Court, a sunset sail on the hotel's catamaran, and duet spa treatments.

Maui ▪ Molokai ▪ Lanai

To enter, please write, in, 250 words or less, how wearing the Harlequin wedding gown will make your wedding day special. The entry will be judged based on its emotionally compelling nature, its originality and creativity, and its sincerity. This contest is open to Canadian and U.S. residents only and to those who are 18 years of age and older. There is no purchase necessary to enter. Void where prohibited. See further contest rules attached. Please send your entry to:

Walk Down the Aisle Contest

In Canada	In U.S.A.
P.O. Box 637	P.O. Box 9076
Fort Erie, Ontario	3010 Walden Ave.
L2A 5X3	Buffalo, NY 14269-9076

You can also enter by visiting www.eHarlequin.com
Win the Harlequin wedding gown and the vacation of a lifetime!
The deadline for entries is October 1, 2001.

Makes any time special ®

PHWDACONT1

HARLEQUIN WALK DOWN THE AISLE TO MAUI CONTEST 1197
OFFICIAL RULES
NO PURCHASE NECESSARY TO ENTER

1. To enter, follow directions published in the offer to which you are responding. Contest begins April 2, 2001, and ends on October 1, 2001. Method of entry may vary. Mailed entries must be postmarked by October 1, 2001, and received by October 8, 2001.

2. Contest entry may be, at times, presented via the Internet, but will be restricted solely to residents of certain geographic areas that are disclosed on the Web site. To enter via the Internet, if permissible, access the Harlequin Web site (www.eHarlequin.com) and follow the directions displayed online. Online entries must be received by 11:59 p.m. E.S.T. on October 1, 2001.

   In lieu of submitting an entry online, enter by mail by hand-printing (or typing) on an 8½" x 11" plain piece of paper, your name, address (including zip code), Contest number/name and in 250 words or fewer, why winning a Harlequin wedding dress would make your wedding day special. Mail via first-class mail to: Harlequin Walk Down the Aisle Contest 1197, (in the U.S.) P.O. Box 9076, 3010 Walden Avenue, Buffalo, NY 14269-9076, (in Canada) P.O. Box 637, Fort Erie, Ontario L2A 5X3, Canada

   Limit one entry per person, household address and e-mail address. Online and/or mailed entries received from persons residing in geographic areas in which Internet entry is not permissible will be disqualified.

3. Contests will be judged by a panel of members of the Harlequin editorial, marketing and public relations staff based on the following criteria:

   - Originality and Creativity—50%
   - Emotionally Compelling—25%
   - Sincerity—25%

   In the event of a tie, duplicate prizes will be awarded. Decisions of the judges are final.

4. All entries become the property of Torstar Corp. and will not be returned. No responsibility is assumed for lost, late, illegible, incomplete, inaccurate, nondelivered or misdirected mail or misdirected e-mail, for technical, hardware or software failures of any kind, lost or unavailable network connections, or failed, incomplete, garbled or delayed computer transmission or any human error which may occur in the receipt or processing of the entries in this Contest.

5. Contest open only to residents of the U.S. (except Puerto Rico) and Canada, who are 18 years of age or older, and is void wherever prohibited by law; all applicable laws and regulations apply. Any litigation within the Province of Quebec respecting the conduct or organization of a publicity contest may be submitted to the Régie des alcools, des courses et des jeux for a ruling. Any litigation respecting the awarding of a prize may be submitted to the Régie des alcools, des courses et des jeux or, for the purpose of helping the parties reach a settlement. Employees and immediate family members of Torstar Corp. and D. L. Blair, Inc., their affiliates, subsidiaries and all other agencies, entities and persons connected with the use, marketing or conduct of this Contest are not eligible to enter. Taxes on prizes are the sole responsibility of winners. Acceptance of any prize offered constitutes permission to use winner's name, photograph or other likeness for the purposes of advertising, trade and promotion on behalf of Torstar Corp., its affiliates and subsidiaries without further compensation to the winner, unless prohibited by law.

6. Winners will be determined no later than November 15, 2001, and will be notified by mail. Winners will be required to sign an return an Affidavit of Eligibility form within 15 days after notification. Noncompliance within that time period may result in disqualification and an alternative winner may be selected. Winners of trip must execute a Release of Liability prior to ticketi and must possess required travel documents (e.g. passport, photo ID) where applicable. Trip must be completed by November 2002. No substitution of prize permitted by winner. Torstar Corp. and D. L. Blair, Inc., their parents, affiliates, and subsidiaries are not responsible for errors in printing or electronic presentation of Contest, entries and/or game pieces. In the event of printing or other errors which may result in unintended prize values or duplication of prizes, all affected game pieces or entries shall be null and void. If for any reason the Internet portion of the Contest is not capable of running as planned, including infection by computer virus, bugs, tampering, unauthorized intervention, fraud, technical failures, or any other causes beyond the control of Torstar Corp. which corrupt or affect the administration, secrecy, fairness, integrity or proper conduct of the Contest, Torstar Corp. reserves the right, at its sole discretion, to disqualify any individual who tampers with the entry process and to cancel, terminate, modify or suspend the Contest or the Internet portion thereof. In the event of a dispute regarding an online entry, the entry will be deemed submitted by the authorized holder of the e-mail account submitted at the time of entry. Authorized account holder is defined as the natural person who is assigned to an e-mail address by an Internet access provide online service provider or other organization that is responsible for arranging e-mail address for the domain associated with th submitted e-mail address. **Purchase or acceptance of a product offer does not improve your chances of winning**

7. Prizes: (1) Grand Prize—A Harlequin wedding dress (approximate retail value: $3,500) and a 5-night/6-day honeymoon trip Maui, HI, including round-trip air transportation provided by Maui Visitors Bureau from Los Angeles International Airport (winner is responsible for transportation to and from Los Angeles International Airport) and a Harlequin Romance Package, including hotel accomodations (double occupancy) at the Hyatt Regency Maui Resort and Spa, dinner for (2) two at Swan Court, a sunset sail on Kiele V and a spa treatment for the winner (approximate retail value: $4,000); (5) Five runner-up prizes of a $1000 gift certificate to selected retail outlets to be determined by Sponsor (retail value $1000 ea.). Prizes consist of only those items listed as part of the prize. Limit one prize per person. All prizes are valued in U.S. currency.

8. For a list of winners (available after December 17, 2001) send a self-addressed, stamped envelope to: Harlequin Walk Down Aisle Contest 1197 Winners, P.O. Box 4200 Blair, NE 68009-4200 or you may access the www.eHarlequin.com Web site through January 15, 2002.

Contest sponsored by Torstar Corp., P.O. Box 9042, Buffalo, NY 14269-9042, U.S.A.

PHWDACONT2

COMING SOON...

AN EXCITING
OPPORTUNITY TO SAVE
ON THE PURCHASE OF
HARLEQUIN AND
SILHOUETTE BOOKS!

*DETAILS TO FOLLOW
IN OCTOBER 2001!*

YOU WON'T WANT TO MISS IT!

PHQ401

TO HAVE AND TO HOLD

Marriages meant to last!

They've already said "I do," but what happens
when their promise to love, honor and cherish
is put to the test?

Emotions run high as husbands and wives
discover how precious—and fragile—
their wedding vows are....
Will true love keep them together—forever?

Look out in Harlequin Romance® for:

HUSBAND FOR A YEAR
Rebecca Winters (August, #3665)

THE MARRIAGE TEST
Barbara McMahon (September, #3669)

HIS TROPHY WIFE
Leigh Michaels (October, #3672)

THE WEDDING DEAL
Janelle Denison (November, #3678)

PART-TIME MARRIAGE
Jessica Steele (December, #3680)

Available wherever Harlequin books are sold.

HARLEQUIN®
Makes any time special ®

Visit us at www.eHarlequin.com   HRTHATHR